LOVE,
NO MATTER WHAT!

LOVE,
NO MATTER WHAT!

Komal Ahuja

Srishti
PUBLISHERS & DISTRIBUTORS

Srishti Publishers & Distributors
Registered Office: N-16, C.R. Park
New Delhi – 110 019
Corporate Office: 212A, Peacock Lane
Shahpur Jat, New Delhi – 110 049
editorial@srishtipublishers.com

First published by
Srishti Publishers & Distributors in 2016

10 9 8 7 6 5 4 3 2 1

This book is dedicated to mothers all over the world who can never stop loving their children, and to all the children who should never stop loving their mothers.

Also dedicated to all those who are struggling for just a little bit of love, simply because they are different.

Acknowledgements

☿

There are a lot of people I would like to thank who helped me in this journey.

My son, *mera noor-e-nazar, meri jaan, mere budhape ka sahara,* my best friend Pranav who said, "Mom this a fantastic story. Please write a book."

Papa saab, who blessed me. *"Mangal ho,"* he said and my phone beeped; it was a mail from my agent saying she is interested. Faith sure can move mountains.

My best friend Shipra, my friend till the end, who read my first rough draft and was all smiles.

Ritu and Shipra for introducing me to Mita, my literary agent.

Mita Kapoor from Siyahi, who trusted me and edited my manuscript patiently, three times over, along with her team members Urvi and Sachi.

My publisher Arup, a honey-dipped sweet Bengali babu who guided me right through and will hopefully be my Krishna in this literary journey.

My husband Lalit, who is a proud husband, encouraging me and loving me always. Though he wonders all the time, *"Tum office mein koi kaam bhi karti ho ya sirf book likhti ho?"*

My in-laws Prabha and Virender Ahuja for loving me the way they do.

My parents Harish and Bharti Bhagat who are my pillars of strength. Their undying belief in me means the world.

My brother Kapil who encouraged me and heard my stories without showing any signs of boredom.

Riya for designing the cover page.

Sanchi, Naveen and Ayush for helping me with the cover designs and being the most amazing friends possible.

Thank you to all my friends and family who encouraged me constantly. I love each one of you.

Thank you for the hundreds of likes on Facebook; they made me smile constantly and strengthened the belief that I can write.

Thank you God for giving me a vivid imagination, sensitivity and this power of expression. People ask me what inspired me to write. I had no inspiration. Just that, one day, God decided to let stories flow out of my mind and my heart.

The birth of Devi

"**I**s it a boy?"

Manish and his parents rushed towards the gynaecologist as she came out of the labour room. "I need to speak to the father in private," she said, not answering the question.

"That's me," said Manish as he followed her to her cabin.

At 30, Manish was a young man. This was their second child after a three-year-old daughter, Khushi. He was a brilliant businessman, who ran a small IT firm. He was a techie, their company made procurement software for the Government of India.

Entering the cabin, he sat down in front of Dr Megha Pathak; Head of the Department of Gynaecology at the Santokba Durlabhji Memorial Hospital in Jaipur. Tension writ large over his face, Manish asked, "What's the problem doc? Are Naina and the baby safe?"

She looked up at him, wondering how to break the news to him. "Both Naina and the baby are healthy, Mr Malhotra."

"Thank God!" said Manish. "You got me all worked up. So tell me what's the issue? As long as both of them are safe, I can handle everything else. Tell me; is it a boy or a girl?"

"Mr Malhotra, we don't know that yet."

"Don't know that? What do you mean you don't know that yet?"

"Mr Malhotra, your baby is an intersex. I have called for the specialists to examine the baby once again. But the way I see it, your baby is not a boy or a girl. It is probably some of both!"

"And what exactly does that mean?"

"Intersex is a genetic condition wherein a person is an intermediate between male and female," replied Dr Megha.

Manish stared at the doctor in disbelief. "But how is that possible? Both Naina and I are perfectly alright. There hasn't been anybody like that in any of our families in living memory. How did this happen? My child, a transgender? I mean why, how?" His voice trailed off.

"The child is not a transgender, Manish; the term I used was 'intersex'. Transgender is an encompassing term which includes everyone who feels or behaves differently from the norms of the gender their anatomy suggests at birth. Let me read this out for you." She pulled out a brochure of the Intersex Society of North America.

"Intersex is a general term used for a variety of conditions in which a person is born with a reproductive or sexual anatomy that doesn't seem to fit the typical definitions of female or male. For example, a person might be born with female genitalia on the outside, but having mostly male-typical anatomy on the inside. Or a person may be born with genitals that seem to be in-between the usual male and female types – for example, a girl may be born with a noticeably large clitoris, or lacking a vaginal opening, or a boy may be born with a notably small penis, or with a scrotum that is divided so that it has formed more like labia. Or a person may be born with mosaic genetics, so that some of their cells have XX chromosomes and some of them have XY."

Manish only half understood what she said or showed; the pain was cutting through his heart like a sharp-edged knife. He sat there still for a few moments, unable to move.

"Who are *Hijras*[1] then?" He asked her after a while.

"The transgender community in India is called the Hijras. In general, Hijras are born with typically male physiology, but identify themselves as women".

"So, now what? What's the next step?"

"I have requested a very senior and one of the best paediatric surgeons in the country – Dr Chaturvedi from Calcutta, you must have probably heard his name – to come and examine the baby. I will take his opinion and then proceed further. Meanwhile, we need to investigate further. I have written a few radiological, hormonal and genetic tests. Please get these done."

"Does Naina know about this?" he asked the doctor with moist eyes.

"No, I did not tell her. I thought it best that you break the news to her," she said getting up from her chair.

Manish had a muddled head, brimming with a thousand questions with not one clear answer.

"One last question doctor. When will Dr Chaturvedi examine the baby?"

---

[1] Hijra is a Urdu-Hindustani word which means leaving one's tribe. These communities sustain themselves by adopting children who are either rejected by or flee from their families.

"He is expected to be here at 4.00 p.m. I shall probably be able to get back to you at around six in the evening and if he agrees, I will ask him to talk to you directly."

Manish thanked the doctor and walked to his parents, who were waiting outside.

He wept on his mother's shoulder as he hugged her. She just waited for him to regain his composure, not asking any questions. "The baby is intersex," he told them.

✕

Manish did not know how he would tell Naina, who had been delighted at the news of the baby. His thoughts kept alternating between her and Khushi as he entered the room where Naina and the baby were resting. *How would he break the news to them? How would he explain?*

He walked in to see Naina lying on the bed looking absolutely exhausted, her eyes shut. His mother was also there, changing the baby's nappy. Naina looked up as he approached and extended her arms for a hug. Manish hugged her back.

She pulled herself away from him and rested her head on the pillow. He held her hand and said, "Naina, I have something to tell you."

"It's a boy right?" Naina asked.

"No, no Naina," he kissed her hand and said, "the baby is an intersex." Naina opened her eyes and looked at Manish; after a few seconds she looked at her mother-in-law. "Please give the baby to me," she said extending her arms. Mithila ji carefully placed the baby in her arms. Naina removed the soft muslin cloth wrapped around the baby and looked at him. She kissed the baby's forehead and then putting her head on Manish's shoulder, wept to her heart's content. He sat there stroking her back and hair, unable to say another word.

Naina was twenty-eight, an alumnus of Mayo College Girls' School and Lady Shri Ram College. A good looking, smart and intelligent girl, she had a petite frame, long black-brown hair and a face that lit up like a thousand lamps. Her parents Mr and Mrs Grover from Delhi were due to arrive at the end of the month. This child was a premature baby, born at the end of eight months and few days. Naina's father was an industrialist and her mother a homemaker.

After a while, Manish took the baby from her and put it on the cot. She lay on the bed and closed her eyes once again.

"Listen, I really have to go to work for a few hours. I'll be back soon. Just rest and take care of yourself and the baby. Call me if you need anything"

He kissed her forehead, looked at his mother and left.

✗

He stepped out of the room, and made his way to the hospital lobby. Settling on a chair, he fired up his laptop, and started looking up 'Intersex'. He was blown away with the sheer magnitude of information available. But the more he read, the more he got confused. His head was buzzing with facts and figures, and all that he had learnt since the birth of his child.

He closed his laptop and walked up to the hospital canteen for a cup of coffee. Maybe this will help me think straight, he thought.

Manish wondered what to do next as his mother walked up to him.

"Maa, what should we do?"

His mother was a homemaker who adored her son and daughter-in-law equally. She lived in her suits, bright formal ones with embroidered dupattas for the evenings, cotton ones for the home. She even wore suits when she slept, no track pants or nighties. "I have something in mind. Just relax!" she said. Manish felt a weight lift off his shoulders. He thanked God for his mother and slowly walked back to Naina's room. He had complete faith in his mother and knew that if she was saying it could be fixed, then it could be.

That evening Dr Megha told Manish that Dr Chaturvedi had confirmed that the child was an intersex and no corrective surgery could be done now as the child was just too small to go under the knife. Once the child turned ten, they could consider surgery.

When Manish broke the news to his father, a retired Superintendent Engineer of Rajasthan State Electricity Board (RSEB) in his early sixties, his instant reaction was, *"Ham logon ko kya kahenge?"*

"Papa what's your problem? What people think about me or not is the least of my concerns right now. I am losing my mind here and you are worried about what we will announce to the world!"

Manish stormed out of the room.

"How dare he talk to me like that Mithila?"

"Will you please relax. How about showing a little bit of sensitivity?"

"But this is also a major concern; the maid, the driver, the neighbours...everyone will ask if it is a boy or a girl? What am I supposed to say? I don't know."

"Pramod ji, let's go home first. Manish will drive us and only Saroj bai ji will be at home. I will handle her"

Three days later, Naina was discharged from the hospital. They had not told anybody about the birth of the baby. No one had even called to check, as the baby was born twenty days before her expected date of delivery. There had been no visits from friends or family, no sweets were distributed, nor was she taken to the Ganesh temple before going home, like they had done for Khushi.

The Malhotras lived in Jaipur, a historical city soaked in the warmth of a colourful culture, the capital of the desert state of Rajasthan. They had bought two adjacent flats on the fourth floor in a new building and converted them into one big home.

A group of Hijras came the next morning; they danced and sang along with their signature clapping outside their flat. They asked Manish's mother to get the baby outside so that they could bless the child. Mithila ji got the baby from inside and handed him over to the Hijras. As she held him in her arms and opened the nappy, she gasped in surprise. They all stopped dancing and one by one came to see the child. Sharmila, one of the Hijras, immediately called Chandani, their Guru on the phone. "Come here quickly," she said and made her note down the address.

They sat down on the floor while Mithila ji served laddus and tea to all of them. Soon an auto rolled up to their building. Chandani, the guru stepped out. She looked a little over forty, and was decked in a bright green sari with a golden border, nails painted red and her hair tied in a bun behind her head. She came and with eager eyes looked at the baby. "Haye Haye!" she said, covering her mouth in amazement. She held the baby and hugged him. She removed some kohl from her eyes and put a small little black *tika* on the baby's forehead. "*Nazar na lage mere lal ko.*" She walked up to Mithila ji and said, "We need to talk." Mithila ji asked her to step inside her house and touched her feet. Chandani blessed her.

Both of them sat in the living room, and without much ado, Mithila ji said, "You may take the baby, but you have to first explain to my daughter-in-law why we should do this. She is an emotional woman and it will break her heart. I beg you to convince her. If you can do that, the baby is yours!"

"Don't worry!" said Chandani, "I'll take care of it."

Mithila ji escorted her to Naina's room. Chandani asked to speak with her alone. As Chandani stepped into the room, Naina got up from her bed to touch her feet. "It's alright!" Chandani said, stopping her, "Don't get up, you need rest."

Naina looked into her eyes knowing exactly why she was there, as Chandani pulled a chair and sat near her bedside.

"I am here to talk to you and I want both of us to talk as matured individuals," Chandani said, breaking the silence.

"I shall try. Please tell me."

"Your child is an intersex."

"Yes, I know that. He is an intersex and an intersex person just has a few genital disorders that can be set right by corrective surgery."

"If you know so much, then I am sure you must have also read that these surgeries don't help much. In fact, they don't help at all. They only result in loss of precious tissue. Go ahead! Open your laptop, read on! I can wait."

"I will not give my child to you. Most of you don't lead happy lives. In fact, your community is marginalized and ill-treated. Very few among you are educated; you do not have safe places to stay either." Chandani let her speak uninterrupted.

"Some of you are sex workers. Have I lost my mind that I will give my baby to a community which will not educate him?

He will probably grow up and dance on the streets and live on the fringes of the society"

"You've had your say, now listen to me and listen carefully. Keep your child if you want to, but he or she will become a psychological mess. I am sure you would not want that to happen. And by the way, how will you address your child? Will you call her a he or a she? Will you name her Radha or will you call him Krishna? Once he grows up, how will you find out which gender does he identify himself with? What if he starts developing breasts, how do you think you will explain it to him? If she identifies herself as a girl and develops facial hair, it will break her heart into a thousand pieces. What will you say to her?

"He needs to be around people who are like him. He needs a support group who understands him and all that he goes through. Who helps him through that entire heartbreaking realization of the fact that he is not like the rest of the world. Loving your child is one thing and accepting him is another. You might love your child, but will you be able to accept him? And even if you do, will your family be able to accept him?"

Naina was quiet, and Chandani smiled a painful smile before continuing, "Do you know what it feels like to be an intersex or a transgender? Trust me, no matter how bright your imagination may be, you will never know what it feels like to be one! The child will have no one to talk to and will turn into an emotional wreck. And who says we are not educated? Quite a few of our kind are educated, and given the opportunity, we would all like to educate ourselves.

"Have you heard of Kalki? She is India's first transgender entrepreneur. Rose works as a communication trainer in one of the leading MNCs in Bangalore.

"Most of the MNCs have a LGBT policy in place."

"LGBT?"

"Lesbian, Gay, Bisexual and Transgender. These are the broader classifications of the queer communities across the world.

"And as far as being a sex worker is concerned, yes, some of us are sex workers, but that is because this cruel world gives us no other choice. We have to make a living, right? We live a decent life, not good, but not bad either; we are a close community and protect each other."

She took a deep breath as Naina's eyes filled with tears again. "I will give your child a normal childhood. I will love her as my own. You can come and visit her whenever you want."

"But who will feed him?" Naina cried, "And who will educate him?"

Chandani got up from her chair and hugged Naina; the two women held each other and shed tears of love and hope. Mithila ji, who was standing at the door listening to the conversation also wept, hiding her tears in her dupatta.

"You will feed her, Naina, and we will educate her together. She will be your baby as much as she will be mine, I promise."

"*Aap promise kariye*, you will take care of my baby."

"I promise my dear girl, I promise." Chandani told Naina that she will leave the baby with her for a few hours every day so that Naina could take care of her and feed her. Naina touched Chandani's feet once again and surrendered the baby to her. She kissed the child's forehead and bid a teary farewell. Chandani blessed Naina saying, "*Bhagwan teri saari muraad poori karega!*"

"The baby is ours!" She announced as she came out of the house. The Hijras danced and sang loudly and played the dhol.

Mithila ji and Naina stood on the gate watching them leave. Naina was happy that at least somebody was celebrating the birth of her baby, at least somebody wanted her.

The Hijras lived in the Haji colony of the Chandpol area in Jaipur. They had a pink kothi with an intricately carved stone work front wall. The kothi had a huge black and golden gate; no footwear was allowed inside. In the middle of the kothi was a small temple of their lord *Aravan*. The Hijras clapped and danced all the way to their kothi from Naina's house, welcoming the child into their fold.

Naina called up her mother that evening, "Maa don't come to Jaipur."

"Why not? Who will take care of the baby? Nani has to be there; in fact, I have bought so many gifts for the baby and the entire family. I bought a beautiful blue crepe suit for Mithila ji and an Omega for Manish ji and."

"Maa, I have given my baby away," Naina cut her short.

"Repeat what you said please."

"I said I have given the baby away."

"When did you have a baby?" asked her mother sounding absolutely shocked.

"Four days back."

"And?"

"The baby is an intersex."

"What does that mean?"

"Look maa, I don't have the energy to go into every detail."

"I am your mother, alright! Tell me everything from the beginning till the end."

Naina told her everything in detail.

"You gave your baby away?"

"Toh aur kya karti maa?"

Mrs Rajni Grover did not answer.

"You are a very strong girl, Naina. I don't know what else to say. How is Manish ji taking all this?"

"I don't want to talk about him. And please don't call him ji; there is nothing ji about him."

"And Pramod ji?"

"You won't believe it but he has been absolutely silent about the whole thing. He has not uttered a word. He is the head of the family. He should have taken a stand".

"Let me come to Jaipur, you have gone through so much."

"What will you do here? The baby has gone away, I gave it up."

"Will you stop blaming yourself?"

"I feel guilty as hell; it was my flesh and blood. What kind of a mother am I ? The one who gave her baby away. Cruel and selfish to the core."

"Naina you did your best under the circumstances, my child. Please don't make yourself miserable. You will fall ill."

Naina could not control her tears anymore.

"Naina, please don't cry. I am coming to Jaipur tomorrow morning."

Naina disconnected the call, buried her face in her hands and wept endlessly.

Devi goes to school

☿

That evening, when Manish came back from office, he went straight to his parents' room. His father turned off the volume of the television as he walked in. Manish sat down next to his mother who told him everything that had happened during the day.

"Mom, I have no issues with what Naina does or doesn't do for the child. But let me make something clear right now; neither me, nor my daughter will have any part to play in this situation. Nobody apart from the four of us will ever know about the baby. I will not stop her from doing anything for that child...as long as I am kept out of it."

Mithila ji got very upset at this attitude of her son. "The baby was not hers alone, so there is no need for you to over-react or punish her. If it was a crime, as you seem to think, you were as much a part of it as she was."

"Mom, you are getting it all wrong here. I am not blaming anybody."

"Then go and spend some time with your wife and treat her properly."

"*Ham logon ko kya kahenge?*" intervened his father.

"The baby was a still born, Pramod ji."

No one reacted to that statement. There was pin drop silence in the room. After a while, Manish walked out.

Naina got up from the bed when she saw Manish walk in. She ran to him, hugged him and cried. He put his arms around her and tried to console her. "It is alright baby," he whispered. "Everything will be alright, just give it some time. Let's go for a drive. It will take your mind off things for a while."

Naina smiled. Manish could always find a way to make her smile. She covered her head with a scarf and slowly walked towards the lift holding Manish's hand. He held her hand even as he drove, but neither of them spoke. She was not sure how he would react if she spoke about the baby and he could not think of anything to talk about. She closed her eyes and all she could think about was her baby. *I wish Manish was man enough to stand by me, probably then we could have kept the baby.*

"So we will abandon our baby just like that?" she asked as she pulled her hand away.

"Look, Naina, I am in no mood to fight, so just don't talk about it. All this has not been easy on me either."

"But I feel guilty as hell. I have not slept a wink since the morning. I sit in bed worrying if the baby has been fed or not. I get visions of the baby crying and no one attending to him."

"Then you shouldn't have given up on the baby. You did not ask me before doing that."

"But your mother did and you said yes."

Manish pushed the accelerator and the car gained speed.

"Shut up Naina! Keep the baby, go get it back now, but remember, nobody will marry Khushi. You want to ruin Khushi's life...go ahead and do it! Jaipur is a small town; nobody will marry your daughter. Do you understand that or you don't?"

Naina did not reply. Manish was angry and was driving the car at a hundred kilometres per hour.

"Will you just slow down a bit, you are scaring me now."

"You talk to me about all that you have on your mind, right now, right here. Let us sort this out once and for all. I don't want to discuss this ever again. Get that and get that clear."

He pushed the brakes suddenly and the car came to a screeching halt. Naina turned around to see if there were any vehicles behind them. He removed Naina's and his seat belts, turned towards her and said, "Speak! I am listening."

"Look, don't raise your voice! I have gone through shit..."

"How about saying *we* have gone through shit? It was my baby too. I was waiting for it. I must have touched your baby bump a thousand times in these nine months to be able to feel it kicking and put my ear against you to hear his hear beat. I am disappointed too, so just stop wallowing in self pity and making a martyr out of your own self."

Naina just looked into blank space.

"And stop putting it on me. Chandani explained to you the whole situation; she convinced you that it is going to be very difficult for us to raise the baby, and that is why you gave it up."

"I gave it up because I knew that you and your family will not support me on this."

Manish took a while to answer. He was searching for the right words to put it across to her.

"Maybe you are right. You promise that Khushi's life will not get affected by this whole situation and I will take you to the Hijras right now and we will get the baby back. That kid's life is already ruined; I cannot ruin Khushi's too."

Nanina was speechless.

After a few moments he said, "You do whatever you wish with the baby. I will not interfere and I won't stop you from doing anything. It's your life and it's your take. I am out of this."

"You disappoint me, Manish. Don't you have a heart?"

"Damn you Naina!" Manish screamed so loudly that it scared her. "You are one goddess, I am not. I am not even human. I am a monster. But I am what I am and I cannot become you. I cannot go on the entire night about this. You think whatever you want about me. I don't care. I don't know a better way to handle this situation. You take it, or leave it."

He turned on the ignition and drove back home, even as Naina wept continuously. On reaching home, Manish turned around and slept, leaving the weeping Naina to sort out her life's miseries.

✗

Next day after Manish left, Mithila ji told Naina about her conversation with Manish the previous night.

"Yes I know, he told me the same thing last night after we came back home. It's alright, maa. The fact that he will not stop me from doing anything for the child is good enough for me."

Mithila ji was surprised at her daughter-in-law's sensibility and maturity.

Naina's mother arrived that morning and spent the next seven days by her daughter's side. She massaged hot oil in her hair twice a day, fed her with her favourite dishes, gave her a patient ear when she needed to vent and held her when she wept. She surprisingly did not ask Naina too many questions.

"Why are you so quiet, maa?"

"I am in my daughter's house, Naina."

Naina did not reply. This one sentence conveyed it all.

"Why didn't papa come with you?"

"Papa is busy with the visa documentation."

"Where are the two of you going?"

"Haven't I told you already? We are going to America to spend some time with Sunit."

"He called me last week, but after that I have not spoken to him."

"So call him up, he is your brother."

"Call him up and tell him what, maa? I just don't feel like talking to anyone right now." Naina closed her eyes; the emotional stress of the past few days was clearly showing on her face.

Chandani kept her word and sent the baby to the Malhotras with Sharmila every day. Rajini held the baby in her arms and kissed its forehead.

"Why has God punished this innocent soul like this?" she said aloud with tears in her eyes as the baby clasped its hand around her finger.

It was time for Naina's mother to leave for Delhi. She tied a pair of Nazarias around the baby's wrists and blessed it.

"I had bought so many gifts for the baby," said Rajni teary-eyed as she hugged Naina.

"So why didn't you get them?"

"I was scared."

"Of what maa?"

"Of how your in-laws would react."

Naina came downstairs with her mother to see her off. "I love you maa, take care of yourself."

"I love too baby," said Rajni as she sat in the car. Naina waited at the door till the car was out of sight and then turned around and ran upstairs to be with the baby.

Naina would hold the baby, feed her and put her to sleep. She would slowly massage her with warm oil; she would bathe her and put on some fresh clothes for her. After a couple of hours, Sharmila would come back for the baby. This routine continued for months. The baby was dropped off at about ten after Manish left for work and sent back before Khushi would come back from school.

Fifteen days after Naina's delivery, friends and relatives began to call to enquire about Naina's health.

"Dadi," yelled Manish's niece into the phone. "When is chachi having a baby? We are all so super excited."

Mithila ji replied, "Nishi, chachi has given birth to a still born baby."

"Oh! Is chachi fine? *Aapne bataya nahi,* we would have been there for her."

"She is fine, just shaken up I guess."

"Is she home, can we come and meet her?"

After that day, the phone did not stop ringing.

Luckily for the Malhotras, they did not have too many relatives staying in Jaipur. Pramod ji belonged to Kota and his family was spread in different cities in Rajasthan. Mithila ji belonged to Delhi and had no family in Jaipur. "Thank God for that," sighed Mithila ji as she answered the twentieth phone call since morning.

Naina just switched off her phone and only spoke to her parents once Manish was back home. She was horrified at the thought of people feeling sorry for the death of her child. She completely blocked herself from the outside world for a while, as if she had gone into hibernation.

When the baby was about eighteen months old, Chandani called Naina and said, "We have decided to name her Chameli."

Naina was disappointed; she didn't like the name at all.

Choosing her words very carefully, she said, "For years, I had a name in mind for my second born. If you don't mind, I would like to name her Devi."

"Devi is a very beautiful name; we will call her Devi," Chandani replied.

"But tell me something, how do you know she would grow up and want to be a woman?"

"I just know. I can read the signs."

Naina didn't ask what signs she was talking about. She let Chandani take a call on this.

Devi was fast growing up. But Naina saw nothing unusual about her. She was a bubbly and innocent little girl. Naina would buy her new toys every now and then. Her hugs and sloppy kisses were the joy of Naina's life.

Khushi too was growing up fast. The kids were three years apart, but Khushi knew nothing about her younger sister's existence. Manish had told her that the baby died at birth and that Mumma would have a new baby soon; and Khushi, all of three years, was smiling within a few hours.

Naina had her hands full with the kids. She ran around the house all day. By the time Devi left, Khushi would be back from school. On festivals, she would always buy gifts for both the girls and Chandani. Manish and she were doing fine; loving and quarrelling like any other husband and wife would.

But one question bothered her continuously. Would she ever be able to send Devi to school?

When Devi turned three, her worry increased. This was the age when children were usually put into play school. But she wondered if any regular school would give Devi admission. Khushi meanwhile had turned six and gained admission into one of the finest schools in town, the Sawai Mansingh School.

The only person outside her family who knew about Devi was Naveen, Naina's best friend from her college days. She decided to speak to him about her worries.

"Naveen, what should I do? I really want Devi to go to school."

Naveen was a simple and happy-go-lucky man, working in the advertising field.

"So what's the big problem? Send her," he replied.

"And what will I say her name is, Devi Malhotra? Manish would kill me if he found out."

"Call her Devi Sharma; let her be my daughter."

Naina was touched at this gesture. How was it that her husband and her best friend were so different from each other?

"Are you sure, Naveen? Won't Srishti object?"

"She is a wonderful lady, Naina. I don't think she will object, and I will definitely talk to her about it. You worry about your husband."

"He has categorically told me that he wants nothing to do with Devi."

"Then what's bothering you?"

"I just don't want any more stress in my life. Which school will take her?"

"Any school would be lucky to have her. She looks like any other girl; nobody will know the difference as long as you don't tell them."

"And her birth certificate, won't they ask for one?"

"Good question. Do you have her original birth certificate?"

"Of course, but that says Baby Malhotra."

"Let me get back to you on this, give me just tonight."

"Thanks Naveen. Take care."

"You too Naina."

Naveen quickly finished his work at the office and called Srishti.

"Srishti, what have you cooked for dinner?"

"Some thin crust pizzas with very little cheese for his Majesty Shree Shree Naveen Sharma."

Naveen laughed. "Thanks, babes. What's the plan post dinner?"

"No plans. Whatever you say."

"You and I are going out for a nice long drive. I will see you in ten minutes. Please start baking; I am hungry."

"See you."

Naveen put the phone down and concentrated on his driving. He reached home in less than ten minutes. He rushed upstairs, changed to a pair of tracks and a lose t-shirt. He reached just in time when Srishti was removing the pizza from the oven. He took it from her hand, sat around the dining table and started eating.

"Why are you in such a hurry? It's piping hot."

"I am hungry."

The family sat together and ate as Srishti served them food.

"Maa, can you please get the kitchen squared up? I want to take Srishti out for a drive."

Naveen's mom replied, "No issues at all. Why is there an urgency in your voice?"

"God! There is nothing you can hide from your mother. Nothing urgent, but it's important. I need to discuss something with her."

"Hope all is well?" Enquired Naveen's father.

"All well. Please don't worry. I will come back and speak to you two also, but before that, I need to get this sorted with her."

Naveen turned around and looked at Srishti. She was busy eating.

"How much will you eat, Srishti? Hurry up. I am waiting for you in the car."

Srishti looked at him amused. "Please give me a paper plate," she yelled.

The maid came running. Srishti took the paper plate from her, put two slices of the pizza, pulled out a tissue paper from the stand and rushed to the car.

She slid beside him and said, "Tell me."

"I am going to tell you something. Don't start judging and jumping to conclusions before hearing me out, ok?"

"OK, I won't."

"It's about Devi."

"What about her?"

"Naina wants to put her in a play school and needs a birth certificate for that."

"Doesn't she have one?"

"Of course she has one, but in that, she is Baby Malhotra."

"So?"

"So the child needs a family name on that birth certificate or she will not get admission anywhere. You know that spineless Manish's stand regarding Devi."

"So how can we help her?"

"I want to give her my family name. Devi sharma?"

"Are you out of your mind?"

"I am not Srishti. I know what I am saying."

"But why would you want to do that?"

"Why not? Devi is such an unfortunate child. Life has been cruel to her. Now she cannot even go to school for the want of a family name, for absolutely no fault of hers. I want to open the doors of education to her. Why shouldn't I help her?

"Do you realize the social repercussions of this?"

"No one will ever know. It is just a name on a piece of paper as far as I am concerned, but for Devi it is everything. Who will try and find out the name of Devi's parents? There are hundreds of Naveen Sharmas in this world and even if they find out, I really don't care."

"But I do."

"What are you worried about?"

"You think your parents will agree?"

"Of course they will. I am sure about it. The only thing they will say is that I should check with you. If you don't agree, they will not allow me to do this."

"I am just not sure about this."

"Come on, speak your mind."

"There is a part of me which is very insecure."

"Really?"

"You share this most amazing strong bond with Naina, and if you give Devi your name, it will become even stronger."

Naveen smiled. "Srishti, how long have we been married?"

"A few years...why?"

"I have known Naina since college, much before I met you. If I had to have an affair with her, I would have had one by now, if that is what you are getting at."

"I never said that. Please don't put words in my mouth."

"Look, I won't lie to you. Naina is my best friend, and yes, I do share this most amazing bond with her. And by the way, it cannot get any stronger than it already is. Srishti, I am not in love with her. I never was. You are my wife. I love you. *Kuchh paak rishte hote hain zindagi mein* even between a man and a woman, ours is one such relationship. She is a happily married woman. Please rest assured and don't doubt my integrity. I promise I will never let you down."

"Ok, one last question. If the baby was not Naina's, would you have still done the same?"

"Of course. It is not about Naina; it is about Devi. Let's do something worthwhile, Srishti. My name on that birth certificate will open a whole new world for her. She will get educated and get empowered. Life is one big struggle for that kid. Let us at least try to make it a little easy for her."

"What if people think it's actually our baby?"

"Oh God! How many times will we talk about this? Let them think what they have to. I don't care. Look Srishti, I have given this a lot of thought. I have a clear conscience and I am not answerable for what I think is right to anybody in this world. I will go ahead and do this with or without you. I beg you to please support me. If you don't, it will make me very very uncomfortable."

"What if Devi thinks you are actually her Dad?"

"Srishti, you are thinking too far ahead. We will cross the bridge when it comes. If she does think like that, I would love to be called her Dad."

"Then she will call me mom?"

"She will not. I promise you that. If that makes you uncomfortable, she won't.

"Alright then. You promise you will love me always?"

"Why don't you make me sign a bond?"

Srishti giggled.

"And sit with me when I explain the whole thing to my parents."

"I will. But I want to have an ice cream first."

"My parents are waiting, Srishti."

"Fine then, you talk to them alone."

"At times you behave like such a kid."

Naveen took Srishti to statue circle, quickly bought her a Cornetto and drove back home.

He went home and had another round of discussions with his parents. Naveen managed to convince them easily. His father applauded him. "I am proud of you, my son. Just make sure you don't hurt Srishti." His mother smiled too. She blew a kiss towards him and said, *"Raja beta mera."*

"See, how well I know my parents," Naveen said to Srishti as they climbed the stairs to their room.

✘

Naveen called Naina the next morning on his way to work.

"Naina, I have some good news for you. Just relax and send the birth certificate to me, and I will send you Devi Sharma's birth certificate tomorrow."

"What will you do?"

"If my name is written on the birth certificate, it means that the baby is Naveen Sharma's...not ours or yours if that is what you are worried about."

"Naveen, all this scares me, but I really want to send Devi to school. What if somebody finds out?"

"Finds out what Naina? If someone sees the birth certificate, they will probably think the baby is mine and Srishti's, and why would somebody want to find out? You just choose the school you want to send her to and fill the admission form."

"Thank you Naveen, thanks for always being there."

The next morning, an office boy came from Naveen's office carrying a big brown envelope for Naina. She opened it carefully and saw a birth certificate which looked exactly like the original, except that the name of the baby was Devi Sharma, daughter of Naveen Sharma.

Naina called him, "Naveen, are you sure we are doing the right thing? If your wife divorces you because of this, don't blame me."

He smiled on hearing her. "Don't worry she won't. We have discussed it at length. We are doing this for a good cause, Naina."

Naina thus put Devi in a playschool which was about half a kilometre from her house. She made sure that none of her friends' kids went there. Saroj baiji,their oldest maid,the only one who knew Devi existed, was put on the job of dropping and picking the child up from school and handing her over to Sharmila who would take her home. Naveen and Srishti attended the parent-teacher meetings as and when required.

Together we shall do it!

☿

Three years went by before they could tell. Once out of play school, all the other kids took admission into the various primary schools of the city. Naina also wanted her daughter to join a primary school like her friends. Devi often asked which school would she go to, but Naina never had an answer for her. She thought of discussing it with Naveen, hoping he would have a solution for her.

"Devi has passed out from play school; I want to send her to a primary school, but I don't know what to do."

"Give me some time to think, and just send a picture of Devi on WhatsApp please."

When Naina sent Naveen the picture, he couldn't help but feel sorry for the little girl. Devi, at six years of age, looked every bit like a regular girl. With her shoulder-length hair tied in a small pony tail, her red checked skirt and white shirt with white socks and black shoes – which was her school uniform – and a small bag hanging across her small shoulders, she looked adorable.

He didn't know what to do to help her, but he wanted to come through for Naina. She trusted him to come up with a solution for her and who else would she turn to, if he failed.

He twisted and turned in his bed all night, unable to sleep. Finally, at six in the morning, he called Naina. "Where are you?"

"Walking in the garden. I couldn't sleep."

"I don't think we should send her to a regular school. I am worried. We might be able to pull this off for a few years, but once puberty hits, I am afraid her appearance might change. And what if she doesn't develop like regular girls do? Girls these days talk to each other about everything, and she just won't be able to relate to them."

Naina was absolutely horrified at this thought.

"What you are saying makes sense Naveen, but I still want to educate her."

"We can teach her, you and me together. Just go and find out the exact course and buy the books. We can teach her all the subjects between the two of us. And listen, please go to the St. Xavier's book shop and get the study material from there, we will follow that school."

"Why Xavier's?"

"Just trust me on this one."

"Thank you Naveen. What would I do without you?"

St. Xavier's was an English medium school run by Christian Missionaries. With its sprawling campus, great teachers and facilities for the all round development of the child, it was one of the most sought after schools in the city.

Later that day, Naina went to the Xavier's bookshop and bought the first standard course material from there. She flipped through them and smiled, it will be a cake walk she thought.

She then called Chandani and put Naveen on conference. The three of them needed to figure out Devi's daily routine.

It was decided that Naveen would take her in the morning for three hours from 7.00 to 10.00, after which she would go to Naina's house, grab a bite to eat and play for a while. Naina would then teach her from 11.30 to 1.30. Chandani was instructed to come and pick her up at 1.45 p.m. sharp because Khushi would return at 2.00 p.m.

Two days after Devi was shuttled between the three houses, she went back home and asked Chandani. "Maa which is my home?"

"Your Mumma's home is your home. Why do you ask?

"And Dad's home?"

"Dad's home is also your home"

"And Naina's home?"

"Now that's not your home. You already have two homes, how many more does a small Devi need?"

Chandani bent down and tickled her, Devi laughed loudly. Chandani always managed to distract her, knowing very well that she will have to give Devi honest answers soon.

Naina's life became absolutely regimented. She would wake up by 6 every morning, go for a half-an-hour walk to the park, complete her morning chores, send Khushi to school and serve Manish his breakfast. Once he left for work, she would quickly take a shower and wait for Devi to arrive. She would feed her and then teach her one subject after the other. By the time Devi left, it was time for Khushi to come home. She would then help Khushi change her clothes, feed her and help with her home work. Time flew like it always did and the first term examinations were announced in all the schools. When Naina heard about this from Khushi, she sighed. She wished Devi could also attend regular school and sit for her examinations like other children.

She was lost in thought when Naveen called.

"Madam, is your student prepared for taking exams? I am sure that Devi will score better in the subjects that I am teaching her."

Naina was shocked. "Wait a minute! Are you saying Devi will be able to take the exams? Which school?"

"St. Xavier's! I know the principal there. Father Peter did not agree at first, but once I made him meet Devi, he couldn't say no. He asked her lots of questions, all of which Devi answered with amazing confidence. She will have to take the exams from the principal's office though, not with the other students."

"When did this happen? And when did you take her to Xavier's? How is it that I never knew about any of this?"

"I am not answerable to you. I am not your husband," he giggled.

"You are impossible, but you are the best!"

Her happiness though was short lived. That night, at the dinner table, her father-in-law said to Manish, "Khushi is nine now. Don't you guys think you should plan another baby? I want another grandchild and Khushi also needs a companion. I am surprised both of you haven't thought about it."

He had mentioned this to Mithila also. Mithila had reacted so strongly that he did not have a choice but to keep quiet about it. "Have a heart, Pramod ji. Naina has her hands full. Her body and her mind need at least a three year gap between two pregnancies to heal," Mithila had told him.

Now that a few years had passed since Naina had delivered Devi, he brought it up again.

This statement struck Naina with the force of a bullet. Her father-in-law was at home every day. He knew very well that she had her hands full with Devi and Khushi. How would she be able to handle another child?

Tears started streaming down her face. She cried silently, scared that somebody might notice. She helped the maids clear the dining table and went to her room. Manish was lying on the bed, flipping through the day's newspaper. She ignored him and went straight to the washroom, undressed and stepped into the shower. As she stepped out of the bathroom ready to sleep, she noticed Manish looking at her, his eyes roaming over her hungrily. But she couldn't care less and plopped herself on the bed, pulled the duvet to cover herself and shut her eyes. Manish reached over to her and put his hand on her waist. She opened her eyes and turned towards him, requesting him to stop. "Manish, please stop it. I am not up for it tonight."

But Manish was too turned on to stop. His hands were now roaming all over her. "Stop it!" She pleaded once again, but Manish was not listening to anything. He thrust his tongue in her mouth to keep her from saying anything, but she kept trying to protest. When he reached down to remove her pyjama bottoms, she screamed a last desperate plea, "Manish, you are raping me. I am your wife. Stop it for god's sake." He was a man possessed and nothing she did could stop him. She could just lie there until he was done.

The moment he was finished, he turned around, hugged his pillow and slept, while she lay there wide awake, still reeling from the turn of the events. She got up and washed herself thoroughly. She kept hoping that she didn't get pregnant as she took another shower and brushed her teeth as if to remove all trace of him. She returned to the room, picked her pillow and made her way to the guest room. She hardly slept that night. She kept thinking about what had happened and how Manish could treat her like that. She wondered if this was the same Manish who always found a way to make her smile.

She woke up the next morning and ran around the house, completing the chores, completely forgetting about the events of the night. Devi and Khushi both had exams coming up and both needed her help. Once their exams got over, life settled into the old routine again. Naina and Manish had also made up after that night. He had come home one night, hugged her and apologised for his behaviour; and Naina like any other forgiving wife had happily forgotten everything.

Naina has a baby

☿

That month Naina missed her period. She didn't know whether to be happy or sad. So she called the only person who could help her sort through her feelings – Naveen.

"Listen, can I come see you?"

"You don't have to ask Naina, just come. Or let's meet up at Cafe Coffee Day, the one near the Deer Park."

"Alright, I will be there in ten minutes."

Naina looked at Khushi sleeping peacefully in her room. She went to the kitchen, asked the maid to watch over Khushi and left.

By the time she reached CCD, Naveen was already waiting for her. Knowing what she liked, he had ordered two tall glasses of Cafe Frappe.

"Hey! What's up?" Naina asked, walking up to him.

Naveen didn't reply. Naina sat down as the waiter came with their coffee. Naveen took a sip and said, "It's Srishti."

"Your wife? What happened to her?"

"She is not being able to conceive. We have been married for ten years now."

Naina felt very guilty hearing him. How did she never notice this? She had been so caught up in her own problems that she never bothered to ask what was happening in his life.

"What is the problem?"

"Ask me what a problem isn't! The mouth of her uterus is tapered, her egg size is unusually small, she has polycystic ovaries and now they are saying she has TB in her stomach."

"Oh! I am sorry Naveen. But all this is curable. Medical science has progressed so much that I am sure there is a way. Or why don't you simply adopt a child?"

"She wants a baby that is truly hers, her own flesh and blood. She is obsessed with the idea of having her own baby and it's getting to me now. If I had it my way, I would have put in my adoption papers years back and had a small child sitting beside me right now."

"You can take mine. I am pregnant," Naina said slowly. "That is what I came to talk to you about. I don't want the baby; it's too much pressure."

"Holy shit! I don't believe this. Are you mad? Where do you have the time to take care of three kids?"

"According to my family, I only have one child. Devi doesn't exist for them."

"You already have no time for yourself. Why did you do this? Don't you have any sense at all? Haven't you and your husband heard of protection?"

"He raped me. I don't want to talk about it."

Naveen fell silent for some time. "But then you should have popped a pill in the morning!"

"That is where I went wrong, Naveen. Both Devi and Khushi had their exams and I completely forgot about it until yesterday when I did a home pregnancy test."

Naveen looked at her aghast. "And are you planning on keeping the baby?"

"Manish wants the baby, my in-laws want the baby; Khushi also needs a sibling."

"I don't understand why you Indian women are so saint-like. You would bloody well die for your families!"

"Even your wife is being silly. If it was me, I would happily go adopt a baby, hug you and sleep every night without a worry in the world."

"Life is so strange, Naina. You are crying because you don't want another baby and I am crying because I want Srishti to have a baby. And oh! What happens if you have another one like Devi?"

Naina stared into space, feeling a terrible pain in the pit of her stomach.

"Naina, I am sorry, I shouldn't have." He hadn't meant to hurt her. It just slipped out. Naina didn't say anything; she couldn't. She knew that was a real possibility.

Naveen paid the bill and they left. He walked Naina to her car and gave her a tight hug, not knowing what to say. She wept as she held him.

Once she reached home, she went to her mother-in-law, sat down next to her and cried. "I am pregnant Maa, but I don't want the baby. What if we have an intersex baby once again? I don't have the strength to go through all of it again."

Mithila ji was horrified. "Please don't talk like that. There is also a strong possibility that we have a normal baby boy who completes the family. Please don't let such negative thoughts enter your head."

"No, but what if the baby is born an intersex? Your son will very conveniently give it up as if it is garbage and I will go through the emotional torture again."

Mithila ji gave Naina some water as she wiped her tears away.

"Look Naina, I understand your fears, but let's just trust God. I know in my heart that you will give birth to a healthy son. This is a chance we have to take, for Khushi and for this family."

"Khushi already has a sister," Naina retorted.

"I know my child, but Manish is how he is. I cannot change him. So for all practical purposes, Khushi does not have a sibling."

"Tell me something honestly, Maa. Would you have accepted Devi as your own if Manish hadn't said anything?"

Knowing Mithila ji would have no answer to this, Naina got up and walked off to her room.

Naina had decided to keep the baby. Manish was delighted while Naveen thought she had lost her mind. He was worried. It was quite possible that Naina would deliver another intersex child, and Naveen didn't think Naina would be able to deal with that. Nine months seemed to take forever to pass. Naina was very scared. She had bought nothing for the baby, not even a single dress. She kept thinking what would happen if she had an intersex child again. Manish had a tough time trying to pacify her and those nine months were sheer torture for both of them.

Naina got busier, now that she also had rounds to the gynaecologist every now and then in addition to everything else. The girls kept feeling her baby bump and asking her innocent questions. One Sunday night, her water broke and a panic-stricken Manish rushed her to the hospital where she delivered a perfectly healthy boy after six hours of labor. They decided to name him Kavish.

The first time Sharmila dropped Devi to school, Father Peter ushered her to the Principal's room. Devi was quite surprised when she was made to sit alone and not with the other kids.

She walked into the house and Chandani greeted her.

"Hello Devi. How was your paper?"

Devi ignored her and walked straight back into the room. Chandani followed her with the plate of her favourite churi, hot hand-crushed roti with lots of sugar.

"Kya hua?"

"I sat alone and gave the paper, not in the class with everybody. I miss my friends. Why can't I sit with everyone else?"

Chandani held her and said, "Because you are a Devi. Do you know the meaning of your name?"

Devi nodded and smiled. "A goddess."

"So a goddess is different from the rest of the world. You are different and you are special...that is why you sit away from everyone."

"Are you different too?"

"Yes, all 34 of us in this kothi are different, that is why all of us stay together."

"And they are all different, so they stay together?"

"Yes, they stay with their families and we stay with ours. We are all one big happy family – Sharmila, Savitri, you me and the rest."

"And Dad?"

"He belongs to the other world, but he loves you."

"And Naina? She loves me too."

"Yes, Naina is also from the other world, and she loves you."

Devi thought for a while, not sure why and how their world was different from that of Naina's and Naveen's as Chandani stuffed some food into her mouth.

"I don't want to sit alone for the exam; you come with me."

"Father Peter is there with you. He is sent by Aravan to help you."

"He comes and goes; he does not speak to me."

"You are not allowed to speak to someone when you take an exam. You are a big girl now Devi and Sharmila waits for you outside. She is right there."

Convinced, Devi continued to finish her meal.

Devi would still come home everyday to study with Naina. She learnt to speak impeccable English, much to the surprise of Father Peter who once asked Devi, how her paper was.

"I was very well prepared, Father. I guess I should score full marks in this test. Thank you for asking."

"That's absolutely wonderful, my child. May I ask who taught you to speak in such perfect English?"

"My father and Naina taught me, Father Peter."

Naveen and Naina had decided that they would talk to Devi in English only. They knew Hindi would not be an issue as everyone else would talk to her in Hindi anyway. This worked as they had hoped and Devi learnt perfect English.

Difficult years

ʏ

Khushi had a normal childhood. She went to one of the best schools in town, had her bunch of friends, celebrated her birthdays, participated in school competitions and went for school trips and family holidays. She got to wear expensive clothes, had a family who doted on her and now a baby brother too.

Devi on the other hand led a very quiet life. She juggled between Naveen's house and Naina's house for her studies and was sent away before Khushi came home. She did not have any grandparents who could spoil her, never celebrated festivals with her family, nor was she a part of the trips they took twice a year. There were no school trips or competitions for her and no siblings either. She spent her evenings with Chandani and Sharmila in their kothi. Her only recreation was the dance classes that Chandani took for everybody in the evening. Her best friends were books and she spent most of her time with them. The only time she went out of Jaipur was when all the Hijras went to Tamil Nadu every year to attend their annual festival in Koovagam.

The festival of Koovagam is held for two days at the Koothandavar temple in honour of the Hindu Diety Aravan or

Iravan. According to Hindu scriptures, Aravan was the son of the Pandav prince Arjun and his Naga wife princess Ulupi. In the *Mahabharata,* he is portrayed as dying a heroic death in the eighteen-day Kurukshetra War. He had self-sacrificed his head to seek the blessings of Goddess Kali to ensure the victory of the Pandavas in the war. Lord Krishna had granted him three wishes, pleased by his sacrifice.

Aravan wished to marry before he died. Krishna changed his form and became Mohini. She spent the night with Arayan and when he was killed the next morning, she grieved like a widow, breaking her bangles and beating her chest. Aravan is worshipped in the form of his severed head and is believed to cure disease and induce pregnancy in childless women.

The transgender devotees from across the country collect at Koovagam every year to re-enact the story of Aravan. In a symbolic ritual, the participants take on the role of Mohini and are married to Aravan by the temple priest. The next day, they mourn Aravan's death with ritualistic dances and breaking their bangles. In addition to the religious ceremony, there are beauty pageants and singing contests. Devi loved every minute of the festival. It was such a riot of colours, a delightful sight to behold.

As Devi grew older, the difference in the life of normal people and herself began to bother her. When she was in the fifth standard, there was an entire chapter in her science book about the human reproductive system. Naina called Chandani.

"Chandani, we need to meet soon."

"We sure will. But is there anything urgent?"

"There is an entire chapter in her science book about the human reproductive system along with diagrams."

"So teach her."

"Chandani, she will have a thousand questions to ask, let's meet and you explain to me how to explain everything to her."

"She will ask you nothing, Naina. Go ahead and teach her everything. She will surely come and ask me and I will handle it. Just make sure you send the book home with her."

This is exactly what happened. Naina taught the entire chapter to her. Devi looked distant and forlorn, but she said nothing.

Devi ran to the house and caught Chandani by her hand.

"I need to speak with you urgently. You leave everything and come here."

Chandani followed her to her room and she shut the door.

"What happened?"

"Look at this," Devi quickly opened the chapter.

"Who am I? A male or a female"

"A female, Devi."

"Look at these pictures, Maa."

She showed Chandani the picture of a male reproductive organ and a female reproductive organ.

"I am a male, Maa . Why do you call me Devi?"

"Look at yourself in the mirror Devi." She handed over a small mirror to her.

"What do you see here?" Chandani asked lovingly.

"A female," answered Devi, absolutely confused.

"How can I be a female if I have a body of a male?"

"Do you feel like a male or a female?"

"I am not sure anymore."

Chandani pointed to the picture of both the reproductive organs.

"You have both."

Devi gasped in surprise.

"And you?"

"I have this," said Chandani pointing at the male reproductive organ.

"But you are a female, you wear a sari."

"I am a female trapped in the body of a man."

"And me? Who am I?"

"You are also a female but you have both the organs. The term is called intersex."

"Naina did not teach me about the intersex. She said there are two types of people in this world – male and female.

"Naina did not say this; the book says so."

"Are we so insignificant that there is no mention of us in the textbook?"

"Not insignificant, but very few in number as compared to them."

"But we are there, we exist. What are we called? Male, female and?"

"The Hijras."

"So they should write that there are three types of people in this world – the males, the females and the Hijras."

"The third gender," Chandani corrected.

"Is this the difference between us and the rest of the world?"

"Yes"

"How does this happen, Maa. Why are we not like everyone else?"

"God simply gets confused sometimes, Devi."

"You mean he made a mistake? He is God. How can he make mistakes?"

"No, my dear child, he created some special people who are not like everybody else."

"You are right; we belong to a different world, and this world is so different from theirs. I am not sure I like that world anymore. There is not even a mention of us in the text book."

Chandani hugged Devi.

"I love you."

"I love you too Maa."

Naina found Devi's teenage most challenging. Her shoulders had become very broad and she was gaining height unusually fast. At 13 years of age, she was already five feet four inches tall. One day, Naina noticed tiny hair on her face, as if she was developing a beard; the next day they were gone. Another day, Naina noticed small breasts under her top when she had looked absolutely flat until the previous day. Devi hardly spoke to Naina and would want to leave the moment she finished her studies. Naina had always bought all of Devi's clothes, but suddenly she didn't seem to like anything that Naina bought. Devi was growing distant every day, and Naina did not know how to handle it.

She called Chandani. "Devi is changing. She doesn't seem to like being with me anymore. It is like a total breakdown of communication between us. Why is she behaving like this? Have I done something wrong?"

Chandani replied very calmly, "She is going through a lot of changes and you will have to be extremely patient with her. Please try not to ask her any questions. It is probably the toughest part of her life. I will handle everything slowly."

"Alright," Naina said and disconnected the call.

One evening, Devi held the end of Chandani's sari and pulled her into her room.

"Who gave me to you? You don't have a uterus. Inside, you are a man."

"God Aravan."

"Will you keep God out of our conversations please? I am a grown up girl."

"Naina...you are Naina's baby."

"I knew it. I just knew it. That is why she loves me so much."

"Does she have a husband? Of course she has one. Wrong question. Do I have a father?"

"Yes, obviously."

"And the man doesn't want me. Who wants him either? I have a dad."

Chandani did not reply.

"Why can't I live with Naina in that big house?"

"You tell me?"

"That man does not let her keep me. Why? Just because I am different from him? But he created me. Isn't it?"

Two tears rolled down her eyes.

"They had fun and fucked up my life," she said sounding absolutely bitter.

She threw her book away. She refused to eat her meals. She sat in front of Aravan and cried. Sharmila tried to go to her to console her, but Chandani did not let anyone go close to her.

"Let her cry till her tears dry. The earlier she accepts reality, the better it is."

That night, when Devi walked back to her room, Sharmila followed her with some food and water.

She held her hand and made her sit on the floor.

"Sharmila, I need some straight answers. I am tired of God being the reason for everything in my life."

"Ask."

"Why are we different? Why can't we live our lives like everyone else? Have a normal life, a father, a mother, a brother and also a baby sister and a house like everyone else? Why are *we* a result of this biological goof up and not others? Is that too much to ask?"

"I don't know why all this happened to us, but I know for sure that we cannot change anything. So why feel miserable and waste your precious tears on something that will not change, no matter how hard we try. The earlier we accept it, the better it is."

Before Devi could react, Chandani walked into the room. Sharmila left quickly upon seeing her.

"Close your eyes Devi," she instructed.

"There she goes again," thought Devi.

She did as instructed. "Now we will count our blessings. You start first."

"Maa, Aravan, our family, Dad."

"And school?"

"Ok, school."

"Is that all? Ok, now I will start. I have Devi, our family and Aravan. I don't have a mother and a father. I don't even have education. Who has more?"

Devi did not reply.

"You also have Naina," Chandani continued. "She, my dear Devi, is your biggest blessing. She did not abandon you for a single minute. She is your mother and I am also your mother. You have two mothers; you are the luckiest of us all."

"Do you miss your Maa?"

Chandani, choked with emotion, gave a barely audible yes.

"Don't worry, I am there for you. I will be your Maa."

Both of them smiled through their tears.

"Can I sleep with you today?" enquired Devi.

"Yes, of course, but I am not sure if both us will fit on that bed."

"We will. I will hug you"

"Alright, but before that, you will have to finish your food."

Devi quickly ate all her food and hugged Chandani and slept.

✗

Devi was in the eighth standard now and Khushi in the eleventh. Khushi was so busy juggling between tuitions, that even she had no time for Naina. Manish was busy with work; he had to provide for his family and he was working hard to give all of them a good life. All of them, except Devi, but at least he never stopped her from doing anything for Devi. Her only source of distraction now was her baby Kavish who had also begun school.

By this time, Naveen's wife had got two artificial inseminations done, both of which were unsuccessful. Naveen even took Devi with him to Alsisar fort. Devi had been super excited about her weekend away. She absolutely adored Naveen. Srishti, though not her best friend, had accepted Devi's presence in Naveen's life.

Devi had a very feminine face and equally fair complexion. She took after Naina as far as looks were concerned – had long, thick hair which fell in soft black curls on her back and very beautiful, expressive black eyes. Her lips had become slightly dark but she always used a light pink lipstick. She had already started getting her eyebrows shaped and the slight hair that Naina had noticed around her chin never appeared again.

Naina had a suspicion that Chandani made sure they didn't. Her hands and legs were always waxed so they appeared squeaky clean, but she was tall, had broad shoulders and a muscular built. The one thing that stood out about her was the confidence that oozed out of her face, which Naina thought might be because of her education. Maybe all the books that Naina and Naveen kept gifting her had made a difference after all. She loved wearing long skirts with tops, the latest foot wear in bright colours, and liked a little bling. Naina had slowly learnt what to buy and what not to buy for her. In fact, both of them would log on to Flipkart and Myntra and buy dresses online.

On her fourteenth birthday, Devi told Sharmila that she wanted to be able to move around alone and did not want to be escorted everywhere. Chandani was very apprehensive about her using local transport, because she was worried about her being unable to handle the lewd remarks or comments being made about her. Devi managed to convince her that she was a strong girl and that she would be able to handle it. When Chandani bought Devi her first cell phone, she was delighted. Devi hugged Chandani and promised to call her in case she needed any help.

From that day, life became an adventure for Devi. She would wake up very early and take the local bus to Naveen's house. Once she finished studying, she would walk to the bus stand to catch the bus for Naina's house. She was happy being on her own. Surprisingly, no one bothered her much, except some people who would look at her in amazement. But she was quite used to that by then. Nobody had seen such a young transgender and one who did not wear the trademark bright saris with heavy embroidery and golden borders, loud make-up and lots of jewellery and bangles.

A young boy would travel in the same bus with her. She saw him sitting on the front seat every day. He would keep looking out of the window and not speak with anyone. He looked like a first-year college student. Devi liked him; he was her first crush. She would always try to get a seat from where she could see him. Just the thought of seeing him would make her smile. One day Naveen noticed that she was smiling more than usual and asked her what was making her so happy.

Devi didn't know what to say. "No dad, nothing at all," she said and continued to smile.

Naveen knew her like the back of his hand and understood the situation. *This girl is going to get hurt very badly*, he thought to himself and prayed that God gave her strength to deal with whatever was in store for her. He knew that there were no teenage or even twenty-something transgender as he had never seen one when he had gone to drop Devi at the kothi. He prayed and wished with all his heart that there was one young transgender he knew nothing about.

One day, Naina called Chandani frantically. "Please make sure that Devi does not come to my house today. Manish is at home and so is Khushi. They are both quarrelling and I don't want Devi to be caught in the middle of it."

Once in a while, when something like this happened, Chandani would always cook up some story and call Devi back. Naina could never talk to Devi about these issues; and what would she say even if she tried.

Devi never asked her any questions about the family and Naina never brought them up herself. She shuddered to think what would happen when Devi found out, or had Chandani already told her everything?

"It is 10.30 already Naina. She will reach any minute now. How do I call her back now? Oh God! Let me try."

Naina heard Khushi shouting in the other room and disconnected the call.

"Why did you have to buy me this phone, Dad? I don't like it. I want an iPhone and that's the end of this discussion."

"I bought this phone for you because I thought it was the best for you. Take it or leave it. I am not buying you an iPhone."

"Fine! Keep it then! And don't complain later that I don't tell you where I am going and don't panic when I get late at a party."

"I don't like the way you are talking Khushi. It is hard earned money, alright? And this is a perfectly fine phone. I don't see what your problem is."

"If it is so wonderful, you keep it."

Manish got really angry at this. "How dare you talk to your father like that?"

"Relax, both of you! We can try to sort this out amicably," Naina intervened.

"You stay out of this Naina. It is because of you that she has become like this. You have had no time to take care of your children. If only you had some values which you could have passed on to her."

Before Naina could say anything, Khushi exploded. "Why are you blaming Mom? This is between you and me."

Mithila ji had been standing quietly all this time holding Kavish; she also spoke up. "Khushi, this is no way to talk to your father."

"Dadi, now you please keep out of it."

"How dare you talk to your grandmother like that?" Manish shouted.

"Fine then, I am leaving. You can keep this phone." She walked out of the room, tears in her eyes.

Manish turned around and started screaming at Naina. "It is all because of you! Why don't you leave us alone and go and stay with those Hijras of yours!"

"Yes, of course. It is all my fault, right? I created Devi alone. You had your fun and then dumped her like she was garbage. You are just a coward Manish! I should go and let you raise Khushi and Kavish alone."

Mithila ji walked out of the room with Kavish.

"You, your mother, all of you are cowards!" Naina said crying hysterically as Manish walked out in a rage.

Discovery

☿

All this while, Devi had been standing in the living room listening to everything. She had hidden behind the guest room door every time she heard footsteps coming towards the living room. She had switched her phone off as she entered the house because Naina hated it if her phone rang while she was teaching. That was why Chandani also couldn't get through to her. She had seen her father and siblings for the first time that day. She had found out that she had a grandmother too. She had a family!

Naina wiped her tears as she left the room. Khushi called her up after a few minutes, "Mom, I am sorry you had to listen to all this because of me."

"It's alright, baby. Dad will be fine soon, but you need to behave yourself. This is not the way to talk to your elders."

"Yes, I know that. But when I specifically asked him to buy me an iPhone and he agreed to it, then he should have bought me one. And even if he decided not to buy it, he should have asked me for another choice instead of getting whatever he wanted."

"It's alright now, forget it. Come home and we'll talk about this. If you have the packaging, maybe we can return it and get you a phone of your choice. But an iPhone is expensive Khushi, you have to understand that."

"I have the packaging; we'll go and return it. Yes, I understand that. I am not asking you to buy me an iPhone. Give me a budget and I will get a phone of my choice within that amount."

"Alright."

"Mom, what was dad accusing you of? Where do you go and spend all your time?"

"I don't remember him saying anything of that sort."

"Of course you do, mom. Anyway, I will not push you. Bye, Maa."

"Bye and please don't spend so much time with Pranay; I don't want another fight in my house."

"You know that I like him, Maa. But I will be careful."

Pranay was Manish's best friend, Nikhil Kapoor's son.

Hanging up, Naina saw that there were three missed calls from Chandani. Worried, she quickly called back. Chandani answered almost immediately.

"Naina, where is Devi?"

"I have no idea. I haven't seen her since yesterday. I thought you were calling her back to the kothi."

"I have been trying to contact her ever since you called, but her phone is switched off. I don't know where she is Naina. I am worried. I hope she is alright."

"Please don't worry, she will be fine. I just hope that she didn't come here."

"I hope not!"

"I will call you if I hear from her. In the meantime, please call Naveen and see if he knows where Devi is," Naina suggested.

Naina ran out of the room and found her maid Saroj in the kitchen. "Saroj, have you seen Devi?"

"She just left about ten minutes back." Naina immediately called Chandani to tell her.

Meanwhile, Devi had left from Naina's house and walked to the bus stand, tears flooding her eyes. There were so many questions running through her head. She couldn't understand why no one had ever told her about her family.

She called Naveen and completely broke down on the phone. Naveen heard her crying at the other end of the line and got worried.

"Please stop crying, Devi. Calm down! Devi, tell me what happened?"

"Devi, are you there? Say something please." Naveen kept trying, but there was no response from her. All he could hear on the phone were Devi's sobs. He was in the middle of a shoot, so he disconnected the call and called Naina.

"What happened? Devi just called and was hysterical!"

Naina told him everything that had happened that morning and asked him if Devi had told him where she was.

"I don't know where she is, but you have to do something. I am in the middle of a shoot; I can't leave. Go and look for her, Naina, and keep me posted please. I am scared that she might do something to herself."

Naina picked up the keys of her car and rushed out of the house. She decided to first check the route to Chandani's house as that was her best bet. She had barely driven for a few minutes when she saw Devi sitting under a tree. Sighing with relief, she parked on the other side of the road and quietly went and sat by her side. Devi looked at her, but did not say anything. She was feeling cheated. Naina did not know what to say; she knew that Devi would have a million questions for her and that it was time to tell her everything. But Devi was not in a frame of mind to listen. She was still very angry.

"Devi, let's go home! Come on, get up darling." Devi did not answer. Naina touched her shoulder and coaxed her to get up again.

"Come on Devi, we cannot sit here forever. I know you have a lot of questions for me and I will answer each one of them, I promise. But let's go home first."

Finally, Devi got up and sat in the car and Naina drove towards the kothi. The moment Naina stopped in front of the house, Devi ran out of the car without so much as a word to her mother. Naina felt tears well up in her eyes as she sat there. She did not know what she would say to Devi. She was thinking of ways to fix the situation when her phone rang. It was Naveen.

"What happened? Did you find her?"

"Yes." Her voice was choked with tears.

"Thank God! I was so worried! Where are you right now?"

"In my car, outside Chandni's house."

"And Devi?"

"Inside the house."

"Okay. Stop crying and go back home. There is not much we can do right now, except answering all of Devi's questions. The damage is done. You won't achieve much by sitting there and crying. Just go back home, alright? I will go and see her once I am done with my shoot."

✗

It was midnight by the time the shoot wrapped up. Naveen called Naina, "I am coming to pick you up. We are going for a drive."

Naina had been fast asleep when he called.

"It is the middle of the night, Naveen. I cannot just go for a drive with you right now. I am a married woman and if someone finds out I am alone with you at this time of the night, I will not have a marriage to call my own."

"I know that Manish isn't in and we need to fix this situation with Devi. Now come out."

"But, what about Srishti?"

"We will take her too."

"Give me ten minutes. I have to inform my mother-in-law."

Naina washed her face, changed her T-shirt and went to Khushi's room to check on her. Then she tip-toed inside Mithila ji's room, careful not to wake her father-in-law or Kavish, who was sleeping between his grandparents.

"Mummy ji," she whispered.

Mithila ji woke up with a start. "What happened?"

"Nothing happened. I am going out for a drive with Naveen and Srishti."

"In the middle of the night?"

When Naina did not answer, Mithila ji said, "Alright, go. But make sure you are back before Pramod wakes up. He will not approve of this."

"Yes, of course. And you have Naveen's and Srishti's numbers too, just in case."

She quickly ran outside, picking up her house keys and carefully closing the door behind her.

Naveen was waiting outside for her. They picked up Srishti and then Devi, who was waiting outside Chandani's house.

"Let's go buy some ice-cream first." Devi's face lit up as they drove to Statue Circle where Naveen bought ice-cream sticks for everyone. They put on the stereo and drove up to Jal Mahal. Naveen told them about his shoot and Devi hung on to every word excitedly. Soon Devi had eased up and all four of them were laughing and singing loudly along with the song from the stereo. *Chaar botal vodka, kaam mera roz ka, na mujhko koi roke,na kisi ne roka!!!*

Naveen looked around, positively amused at the women around him. "What kind of a song are you guys singing? I like the way you're all singing it together as if it is some kind of a family anthem. Earlier families would get together and sing motivational songs like *Itni shakti hamien dena data.* Look what the world has come to now." Naveen sighed and everyone burst out laughing.

They drove around for two hours. Naveen took them to the Amer Fort and then up to Nahargarh. Jaipur is a beautiful city and the midnight drive was breathtaking.

On their way back, they dropped Devi first. Naveen pulled up in front of Chandani's house and before Devi could leave, he said, "I had a brilliant time, guys. Thank you so much. I feel absolutely blessed to have all of you in my life. Life is short and at times can be really cruel, but we must learn to count our blessings and keep moving forward."

He got out with Devi to escort her to the door. Naveen put his arms around Devi and gave her a tight hug before she could go inside.

When he came back to the car, he said, "Devi says she wants an iPhone. I will buy her one tomorrow, if that is what she wants, but I don't understand where this is coming from. I mean she has never ever asked me for anything before."

Naina told Srishti and Naveen about the fight between Khushi and Manish which Devi had overheard. "I will buy an iPhone and send it to you tomorrow, Naveen. I have some money saved up."

"She did not ask *you* for a phone, she asked *me*. So just chill! And I can easily afford to buy an iPhone. Ask my wife here if you doubt me."

"Yes Naina. Naveen can easily afford to buy an iPhone for Devi. So don't worry."

"I can afford to buy one for you also Srishti, if that is what you are implying. I'll buy one for you also, ok?"

"Yes! Naina, you are my witness just in case he feigns ignorance tomorrow."

Naina closed her eyes as Naveen and Srishti kept pulling each other's leg. She thanked god for everything. When Naveen finally dropped Naina home at three in the morning, she went to bed relieved and happy.

A broken heart

♃

Devi did not ask Naina any questions after that day. Chandani had explained everything to her.

"I have a brother, a sister, grandparents, everyone Maa, and no one told me about them ever, not even you."

"What would you do even if I did tell you about them? It would just cause a lot of pain."

"So it's hurting even now."

"Get used to all this Devi. We have gone over this a thousand times now. You are ours; our world is different from theirs. You are lucky, you have Naina, Naveen and Father Peter around you. They are godsent. "

Devi put her arms around Chandani. "It's a cruel world out there Maa. I am happy to be here."

Naveen bought her a new iPhone 5S and she was delighted. All the bitterness was forgotten. Devi continued to look at the boy in the bus and smile thinking about him. One day, she saw that the front seat where he normally sat was empty. In fact, most of the seats were empty that day. She wondered if it was some kind of holiday. She went and occupied her usual seat and put on her earphones. The bus stopped at the next stop and a few more people climbed in. One of them came and sat right next to her as she was gazing out of the window. She turned around to see that it was the same guy who made her heart skip a beat. As soon as their eyes met, he cringed in disgust. He immediately got up and went to sit on an empty seat near the back door. Devi's heart broke into a million pieces. Fat tears rolled down her cheeks one after the other. She was on her way to Naina's house to study. She reached the house and found Naina waiting in the guest room, geography textbook in hand. Devi was in the ninth standard now; her studies were getting tougher every day. Naina had to first understand the chapters herself and then teach her. Devi now came to Naina's house only twice a week with her problems, rest she would study on her own. Naina looked up from the book when she heard Devi enter. "Hi Devi, how are you?"

It took a lot of effort for Devi to smile in return. The look on her face was enough to tell Naina that something was wrong. She got up, put an arm around Devi and said, "Tell me what's bothering you, my dear." Devi held her and wept profusely. Naina let the tears fall and stood there, her arms tightly embracing her.

"Devi, sit down and tell me about it."

"Why doesn't anyone like me?" Devi wailed. "My entire family and even that guy on the bus. No one likes me, why mom, why?"

Naina knew that it was time to tell Devi everything. She could not avoid that conversation any longer. Naina thought Devi was old enough to understand and accept the facts, no matter how cruel they were.

"Sweetheart, what I am about to tell you might hurt, but the sooner you accept facts, the better it will be."

Naina poured her heart out to Devi. She told her about what had happened when she was born and her meeting with Chandani. She told her why Naveen and she had decided to not send her to a regular school. She told her of the various prejudices that the society had against the transgenders. "I have never told the world that you are my baby; never even let you use your family name. All of it was because of Manish alone or the pressure from the family; and also because I have to get Khushi married someday. No one will marry your elder sister if they find out that her mother gave birth to an intersex child. Your sister would never have found a companion and I couldn't let that happen. I love all three of you equally. I never told you about the family because it would have hurt you. Your grandparents and your father are far too set in their prejudices against people like you to change. It's culturally engrained into their systems and it will take a long long time to change that. I love you sweetheart, I always have; but there is only so much I can do for you. You will have to fight your own battles. I can only hope to make you strong enough for that."

Devi got up and hugged her as they both stood there crying, with arms tightly wrapped around each other for quite some time.

"There is one last thing that I have to say to you Devi and I want you to listen very carefully. I don't want you to ever sing and dance on the streets; you are made for bigger things in life, Devi. Always remember that."

Naina wiped her tears and said "Come, I will teach you how to make some pasta. You love that, don't you?"

"Yes. I would love that, but what about geography?"

"Don't worry, I will teach you before you have to leave. We still have plenty of time."

"Before Khushi didi comes home." Devi completed the sentence for Naina. Naina smiled, relieved that she didn't have to lie to Devi anymore.

"I promise you, I will tell Khushi about you the day she gets married."

Devi smiled. "Then she will probably quarrel with you about why you hid all this from her the entire time. And you will have to give her an explanation like the one you gave me today."

Naina took Devi's hand and walked her to the kitchen.

"Alright, pasta time now! First, you boil the water and add a few drops of oil and a pinch of salt..."

As Naina and Devi bonded over pasta, Mithila ji, Pramod ji and Kavish played ball inside the closed bedroom door, unaware of what was going on outside.

Soon, it was April and the new session had started. Devi was now in the tenth standard and Khushi had gotten admission into Miranda House in Delhi. She had left for college and Devi had started studying in earnest from day one itself. The only subject she was weak in was Maths. Naveen had managed to teach her Math till now, but she needed to have a tutor if she wanted to clear her Math board exam. They approached one tuition centre after another, but they all refused to let Devi sit in their class. All the good teachers were taking their own batches of students during the evenings, so no one was free to come to Naina's house and teach Devi.

Devi scored five out of ten in her first Math class test as opposed to nines and tens in all the others. One day, while Naveen was talking to one of his clients from London on Skype, it stuck him that they could simply put a webcam in the tutor's room and Devi could attend the classes without being physically present. He quickly called the tutor who ran a tuition centre next door from his house with the idea and as luck would have it, the tutor agreed. He was a Tamilian and an absolute master of his subject. It was decided that Devi would sit in the adjacent room and attend his class through the webcam. After each class, he agreed to give Devi fifteen minutes so that she could clarify any doubts that she may have. The system worked pretty well. The tutor would answer all her questions, but he was always very rude to Devi.

Chandni and Naina both started taking extra care of her nutrition. Devi had stopped going to Naina's house completely now. Naina would drop in from time to time with something or the other for Devi to eat.

Very soon, it was time for Devi to take the pre-board examinations. She scored ninety-one percent marks, but her Math scores still had room for a lot of improvement. The pressure was increasing every day and Naveen and Naina were doing all they could to help her. With fifteen days to go for the exams, the list of the centres assigned to students was announced. Thankfully, Devi's centre was St. Xavier's itself. Naveen heaved a sigh of relief. He had been worrying himself sick thinking about how they would manage if she got assigned a different centre.

One day, at the Maths tutorial, the tutor came to her room after the batch of students had left. "Devi, ask whatever you want to quickly. I don't have much time darling."

Devi could not believe her ears, *did he call me darling?* She ignored it as he pulled a chair and sat down beside her. He put one hand on the table and with the other hand adjusted his crotch under the table and started solving her problems. After a while, he put his hand under the table again and started fiddling with his penis. Devi did not notice as she was busy flipping through her Maths book, trying to find the sum she had marked the night before. Suddenly, he stood up, opened his trousers and let them hang on his hips as he pulled his hard, erect penis out of his underwear. Devi did not even have time to register what was happening when he caught hold of her hair and thrust his penis into her mouth.

"Lick Devi, lick me," he whispered. Devi felt choked. She wanted to vomit. "Devi, this is my payback for teaching you. Now lick me darling." Her mouth was so full of his penis that she couldn't even shout. He tightened his grip on her hair as she struggled to break free. She looked desperately around the room for something to defend herself with. But there was nothing she could use. Devi's mind was racing. *My teeth!* She put her hands on his thighs, her legs on his, and in one swift move, pushed him away with all her might as her teeth dug into his penis.

He growled in pain and crumpled in a heap on the floor. She picked a chair up as he shouted, "You Hijra, you bloody sex worker! You will fail in your paper!" She hit him hard on his head. She picked up her books and ran outside to Naveen's house next door. Naveen was in the driveway, ready to leave for work with Srishti standing by his side. Devi ran up to him and hugged him. "Dad! Dad!" She cried as she collapsed on his feet. Naveen helped her to her feet and asked Srishti to get some water. Devi held on to Naveen, not letting go of his hand. "He is coming after me, dad."

Naveen looked over her back but saw no one. "Who, Devi? Who is coming after you?" Naveen took her inside the house, shut the door and made Devi sit on the sofa. "Calm down Devi, nobody will harm you. You are safe here." Naveen tried to pull his hand away but she held on tightly, refusing to let go. "Whoever it is, we will take him to the police, don't worry." That scared Devi even more. She had heard about how the police harassed transgenders.

"No police!" she screamed, "Please don't call the police."

Naveen was perplexed. "Alright, no police. Relax Devi, I won't let anyone touch you." He kept asking her what had happened but Devi did not say anything. She did not know what to say to Naveen. When he finally asked her if she wanted to be dropped home, she said yes. Devi kept looking behind her back, as if worried that someone was following them. Naveen knew she was terrified about something, but could not understand what had happened.

He called Chandani and asked her to reach the kothi. Naveen told Chandani what had happened before he left. She asked him not to worry and told him that she will call when she figures out what the problem is.

She rushed inside and found Devi bent double over the wash basin, brushing her teeth. Her worst fears had come true; someone had abused her sexually. The question was, who?

Chandani kept asking Devi to tell her what had happened but Devi refused to talk to anyone for days. All she said was that she did not want to study or sit for any exams. She did not want to see anyone from the other world ever again.

Devi could not sleep that night. Sharmila was asked to keep a close eye on her.

Devi kept twisting and turning in bed. She was angry, very angry. "*Kutta, kamina saala.* He didn't touch all the other girls that came to him to study. He only found me. Why? Because he thought I was alone. Bastard. Doesn't he have daughters himself?"

After a while she woke up in cold sweat. She saw Sharmila sleeping peacefully on the floor, without even a sheet under her. She tiptoed outside the room and went to fetch a glass of water. As she was crossing the hall, she saw the picture of Aravan. The lights around it shining brightly.

She went and sat in front of him and closed her eyes.

"Why did you do this to me? I need an explanation today. You have given me a tough life. I have struggled right through. You are a God. Aren't you supposed to be fair to all? I have a mother but she is not mine. I have father who doesn't want to see my face. I have a family who wants to do nothing with me. In spite of all this, I did not complain to you. I smiled through my tears. You are cruel. You will not be happy until you don't break me totally.

"You first gave me a body that was different from the rest of the world. It is a miracle that I manage to smile. Then you gave me a mind which just doesn't understand numbers. I hate Maths. What are you punishing me for? What have I done? I was only trying to learn Math and now this? *Kya chahiye mujhse?* Why don't you just kill me? I beg of you now, please just stop this cruelty. I will die. I cannot take this anymore. Punish that tutor. Why me?"

Devi started weeping so loudly that the entire kothi woke up. Sharmila woke up, put an arm around her and wept with her. "Enough! Devi enough! We are all with you," she consoled her. Everyone just sat there and watched helplessly. They were not even sure what had happened to her.

Chandani was a worried mother. Her daughter was hurt and she did not know how to help her. A few days later, she walked up to her room and put her arms around Devi.

"Let me help you, my child," she begged. Devi broke down and amidst loud sobs told her everything. Chandani was amazed and asked her why she had not said anything all these days.

"A long time ago, I had overheard a conversation between Savitri and you. You were shouting at Savitri because she had gotten in trouble with the police."

"Who asked you to get into trouble with the police?" Chandani shouted at Savitri.

"He pushed me while we were trying to get into the street opposite the Durgah. What was I supposed to do, smile at him?" Savitri retorted.

"He pushed you because you were breaking the rules! I don't see why you were trying to enter the no entry zone?"

"Because everyone else was entering, and he wasn't stopping anyone else?"

"With that attitude, I am glad you spent the night in jail. The next time you want to do something like that, do it when you are alone, not when you are with the guests. I had sent the Khwaja siras[2] with you hoping that you will treat them with respect and take them to the Durgah. But what did you do? You got in trouble with the police when I have warned everyone a thousand times to stay away from them. I was so embarrassed when they had to come back by bus."

"But I treated them very well and with all due respect."

---

[2] Khwaja siras are Hijras from Pakistan.

"Yes, but they were humiliated and had to fend for themselves in a foreign land just because you could not control your anger? And by the way, how did you manage to get out of the jail in just one day?"

Savitri had kept mum.

"You spent the night with the policeman, didn't you?"

"I could have killed him when he came to me at night, but I didn't."

"Good you didn't, or else your body would have been lying unclaimed at the morgue like Salma's. Or have you forgotten what happened with her?"

"Yes you are right, no one cares whether a Hijra lives or dies. The police are meant to protect the citizens of the country, why do they harass us so much? Aren't we also citizens of India?" Savitri had started sobbing.

Chandani was stunned when Devi recounted the conversation. She was shocked at how clearly Devi remembered every word.

"Devi, my child, I am your mother I will always be there for you and for everyone in this kothi. Remember that always. The police does not help us and its best to stay as far away from them as possible. But this teacher, I will teach him such a lesson that he will never even look twice at another girl."

"You did not reply to Savitri's question that day but I want to know. Why does the police not help us?"

Chandani gave the question some thought, figuring out how best to answer it.

"The police do not help us because they probably don't have a conscience. I hate all of them. Also because there are not too many laws in our favour and whatever few exist are not enforced. A lot of responsibility of this anarchy also lies with us because most of us are uneducated and don't understand the laws. We don't raise our voice against injustice."

Devi was silent as Chandani hugged her and said that she should sleep. Chandani took slow weary steps towards the door and left Devi's room. Devi sat there perplexed, trying to absorb all the information Chandani had given her.

Revenge

Chandani was furious; she called Sharmila and said, "I want every a one here in half an hour. We have to teach someone a lesson." Word spread like wildfire and in half an hour every one of them was standing outside Chandani's kothi. She told them what had happened. "Go and break every bone that tutor has in his body, smash the tables and chairs. There should be nothing left of his tutorial once you are done. But do it carefully. I don't want any trouble with the police."

They went and dressed up like they did for a *badhai*: they wore bright saris, put on heavy makeup and carried their dhol with them. They got into autos and gathered in front of the tuition centre within ten minutes. First, they went to Naveen's house, next door to the tuition centre. They danced and sang loudly and played the dhol in the driveway. Srishti was surprised. She stepped out and asked one of them, "What brings you here? We are not celebrating anything."

"We have come to bless you and your children, my dear girl," Chameli, one of the Hijras told her.

"You have got the wrong house," she yelled, trying to make herself heard over the loud singing. "I don't have any children." But they continued to dance.

"That is not possible, my dear girl. Of course you have children. Now go inside and get some *bakshish* for us."

"That I will give you, but I am not lying."

Sharmila noticed Srishti arguing with Chameli and came towards them. She raised her hand and asked everyone to stop. "Are you Naveen's wife?"

Recognizing her, Srishti said, "Yes, I am Srishti. And you are Sharmila, right? You take care of Devi."

"The lady says she has no children, she does not want to give us *bakshish*."

"Everybody, we have the wrong house, let's leave!" Sharmila shouted.

Srishti handed them a five hundred rupee note as *bakshish*. But they refused to take it and left. They moved next door to the tuition centre, held hands, formed a circle and started dancing and singing and played the dhol. They even caught hold of random passers-by and made them dance along. Very soon, a huge crowd collected around them. The Hijras were giving their best performance ever.

Sone sone patole lakkhan, sone sone patole yeah!! The crowd whistled and clapped their hands to the music. It was around 2.30 p.m.; the last batch of students from the afternoon session had left and the next batch was to come in at 5. Mr Iyer, the tutor was about to leave when Sharmila and Chameli walked in. They had two sticks, each about two-feet long which they had hidden underneath their saris. Chameli went on a rampage; she hurled abuses and threw everything around. She flung the chairs, smashed them against the wall and toppled the tables while Sharmila hit Mr Iyer with a vengeance. "*Kutta saala*," and she hit him with the stick on his legs and hands. He kept begging for mercy until she hit him on his groin, hard. He winced in pain as she hit him again.

They looked around the tuition centre checking to see if they had left anything intact. They came out of the building and quickly joined the crowds. The dancing was in full swing; the crowd was enjoying themselves thoroughly. Chameli came and danced right in the centre, making sure everyone noticed her.

Main ki dassan apni ve, Ae chan karda hai tareefan, Ho mere husn de kone....kone kone di, Hun baby doll mein sone di,baby doll mein sone di.

Sharmila then gave the final performance to a lot of whistling and resounding cheers. Seeing the commotion, the police showed up, but Sharmila was in full swing; she caught hold of a policeman's hand and pulled him in the centre. *Pardesi mere yaara, vaada nibhana, tum yaad rakhna kahin bhool na jaana.* The policemen tried very hard to not smile, but failed to do so miserably. They grinned ear to ear and asked the Hijras to pack up. Sharmila and the others stood in three straight lines and folded their hands in Namaste, while one of the Hijras spread out her pallu and collected bakshish from the cheering crowds. The police sent everybody away and the Hijras went back to the kothi.

Sharmila and Chameli had become heroines in their community. They discussed the incident over and over again the next morning.

"And I hit that Iyer hard where it hurts the most. I hope he dies," Sharmila was showing off.

"But what amazed me the most is that even the policemen were kind that day. They did not shout or hit or use any kind of force," said one among them.

"It was the power of our *latka-jhatkas,*" remarked another, "that turned the hot-headed policemen into patient grinning souls."

Everybody laughed loudly, thoroughly enjoying the conversation.

Chandani called up Naveen and Naina one by one and told them what had happened with Devi and of her decision to not study any further. She also told them that Devi had finally accepted that she belongs to the world, of transgenders and did not want to meet anybody from the other world, except Naveen. She also told them that Devi had not opened her books since the day of the incident.

Naina was at home when Chandani called her. Khushi had come back from Delhi for the weekend and gave in to her curiosity when she saw her mother go to the guest room in a hurry to take the call. She followed her mother and quietly stood outside the door, but she could not understand anything from what she heard. She only understood the name Devi and something about the tenth board exams. But Naina's world seemed to have collapsed around her. She sat down on the bed and started weeping. Khushi walked into the room and shut the door behind her. "Mom? What is the matter?"

Naina didn't even think twice before telling her everything. Khushi was nineteen now, an adult. Naina was sure she would be able to handle it. She summarized the whole story as much as she could, and told Khushi everything.

"I have a sister? And you managed to hide her from me all this while? Mom, I want to see her now. Wait a minute, is she the Hijra you teach at home?"

"Yes, have you seen her?"

"No, no, I heard about her. One of my friend's mother said to me one day that your mother is one hell of a woman. She teaches the Hijras. She called you an amazing human being. I was so surprised. I came home, you were not at home. I asked Dad about it and he simply told me that you do teach two or three of them. He answered so indifferently as if it was no big deal. I did not pay much attention and later completely forgot about it. Maa, I want to see her, let's go."

"I don't think she will meet you Khushi, she is extremely upset."

"She will talk to me. Just trust me and take me to her."

Naina gave in and drove Khushi to Chandni's kothi. They saw Naveen's car already parked on the side.

They entered to see Naveen standing in the hall, facing Devi with a few Hijras including Chandani, standing by the side. He was looking very angry. Before Naina could say something, Naveen had slapped Devi across her face. "Who the hell do you think you are?" he said loudly. Naina was shocked; in all the years she had known Naveen, she had never seen him so angry. "Every time something goes wrong, you decide you don't want to talk to Naina again. And I have had enough of this bullshit. Look at her," he said and pulled Naina by her arm to make her stand in front of Devi.

"She has fought for you against all odds, against her entire family. She has given you everything you could ever need. She had the courage to stand up for you. Ask any of them," he said, pointing towards the Hijras, "Ask them if they know who their parents are. Chandani, tell her. Come on, tell her your story. As a matter of fact, even I want to hear it."

Naveen was in such a rage that no one dared to argue with him. Everybody sat down and Chandani told her story. "I was born a boy. But as I grew up, I enjoyed being in the kitchen with my mother much more than playing cricket with the boys outside. Bright colour dupattas attracted me; I loved nail paints and lipsticks and all things feminine. At night after everybody slept, I often used to take my mom's clothes and dress like a girl.

"My friends started making fun of me. My mother laughed it off. But my father did not take this teasing kindly. He would often tell my mother that she had given birth to an unnatural child. I had an elder brother. One night, he woke up and was horrified to see me dressed up in mom's things. He immediately went to our father and told him what he had seen. I got scared and was hurriedly changing into a shirt and trousers when he came with a stick in his hand. Both my brother and father beat me till I was black and blue. I kept crying and my father did not stop. He kept saying, '*Tu mard hai...Mard ban ke reh.*' My mother tried to save me but he hit her too.

"I got so scared that I hardly went home after that. I would only go there to eat, staying outside the rest of the time. It was tough not being myself. I longed to be with the girls and did not enjoy the company of boys. I had become an absolute loner. Then one day, I saw a group of Hijras while I was sitting on the banks of the river alone. I knew that I belonged with them the moment I set my eyes on them. I told them about my plight and they said that I could spend as much time as I wished with them.

"They explained to me that they were *Ardhnarishwars*. Ardhnarishwar is a combined form of Lord Shiva and his wife Parvati. It represents the synthesis of masculine and feminine energies. I loved their bright saris, their singing and dancing. One day, my brother saw me with them. A neighbour told me that my father and brother were looking for me, sticks in hand. I ran from there empty-handed and kept running until I reached the railway station. I boarded whatever train was standing on the platform. Destiny brought me to Jaipur. Famished and thirsty, I spent days on the street until one day I spotted a group of Hijras, who took me in their fold. I haven't seen my family ever since."

"And have you ever gone to school Chandani?" Naveen asked her.

"We were poor. My father could never afford to send us to school."

"What about after coming to Jaipur? Didn't you ever think of joining school or studying?"

"Which school would have let someone like me inside their classroom?"

Naveen turned around and asked all the Hijras, "Has anybody here ever been to a school?" Everybody shook their heads. "And here is our Devi, who says she doesn't want to study anymore. Everybody clap for her."

Devi had started crying, "Dad! I am sorry."

"Did you ever wonder how I became your dad, Devi? How did Chandani come into your life? It was all because of Naina. As for sexual abuse, it happens to normal girls and boys also. I am proud of you Devi, you are a strong girl. Don't let one freak incident make you quit studies. All of us sitting here have high hopes from you. So stop this drama and get back to your studies."

"But I don't know Math, dad. I will not even get a sixty percent on it."

"Naveen uncle, I will teach her Math," Khushi spoke up.

Everyone turned around to look at the alien face. Recognizing her, Devi spread her arms and Khushi hugged her.

"How did you recognise me?" Asked Khushi surprised.

"How can I not recognize you?" replied Devi with moist eyes.

It was at that moment that Srishti entered. "Naveen! You are here. I have been calling you for like a half an hour. I was getting worried about you."

Naveen looked at his mobile, and found seven missed calls from her. He smiled apologetically as Sharmila whispered something in Chandani's ears.

The Hijras made Naveen and Srishti sit in front of the temple and each one of them came and blessed the couple. "May God give you a happy healthy child soon. *Tumhari har muraad poori ho!*" Chandani then gave Srishti a small twenty-five paisa coin and asked her to keep it with her at all times. Sharmila sat down and tied a black thread on Srishti's arm. Naveen and Srishti touched Chandani's feet and took her blessings.

Soon everyone left, leaving Naina, Devi and Khushi alone to talk.

"Didi, there are only ten days left for my exams. I really don't know much and how will you teach me? Don't you have to go to college? And your father? Won't he be upset?" Devi said to Khushi.

"Devi, I will manage all that. You just concentrate on your studies. I will come from tomorrow morning and teach you. Till then keep your spirits high."

"Why did you come to see me, di?"

"Why wouldn't I come to meet my sister?"

Khushi hugged her once again and both of them shed tears.

"I am sorry you had to go through all this alone. I wish we had each other right from the beginning," said Khushi.

"It's never too late. Now that you are here, I feel blessed."

They sat together and chatted for a while.

The three of them hugged as Khushi and Naina got up to leave.

"Didi, please don't get into any kind of trouble because of me."

Khushi smiled and said, "I won't."

"How did you manage to hide her from us for fourteen years? I can't imagine the stress you must have had," Khushi said to Naina on their way back from the kothi.

"What choice did I have? Your father has never even looked at her; your grandparents don't want anything to do with her. I was given clear instructions that if I wanted to keep seeing her, I had to ensure that you and your father be kept as far away from all this as possible. What was I supposed to do?"

"She came to the house so often, didn't any of your friends or neighbours or the servants ever ask you about her?"

"The servants, no. Only Saroj baiji knows that Devi is my child because she was there when I brought Devi home from the hospital. My friends and neighbours did question me initially, but I told them that I was doing my bit towards the society by teaching Devi. They thought I had gone crazy, but the explanation worked because I never took Devi anywhere with me publically. Eventually, everyone started appreciating what I was doing for Devi as 'social service'."

"Kavish and I got everything from the two of you while all that Devi got was pittance and that too for no fault of hers. This is so unfair."

"Who said life was fair?"

"Now what, mom? Do you want me to live this life of pretence too?"

"You have no other choice, Khushi. Nobody will marry you, and trust me when I say that, if they find out that your mother gave birth to an intersex child."

"Is that possible?"

"Biologically, anyone can give birth to an intersex child."

"Mom, I love Pranay. He is not like that!"

"Oh, for God's sake Khushi! He is an Indian, and so are his parents and his whole family. Even if they were not Indians, they wouldn't agree. Why blame India? People all over have a strong bias against transgenders. If he won't object, his parents will. If they won't object, which is most unlikely, his grandparents will. Why do you want to cause all this stress and pain in your life?"

"But mom, that's so unfair. I hate the idea of lying to dad."

"Then tell him the truth and he and I will fight for the rest of our lives."

"How can you love a man who could not accept his own child?"

"Even I have not accepted Devi in front of the world, Khushi. I can't hold it against him. He has his biases. But more than anything else, he loves Kavish and you. He wants to protect the two of you as much as he can. And he has never stopped me. I have spent a whole lot of money on Devi, but he has never once questioned me about it. Once in a while he does talk very rudely about Devi, but I deal with it. If he wanted, he could have stopped me from meeting her or bringing her home, but he didn't, for which I am grateful."

"She is so pretty. I never expected that, honestly. I mean, most of them are a sad cross between a man and a woman, but Devi has beautiful and soft fair skin, your looks and lovely long hair. And she was standing out among all of them; she doesn't even dress like them."

"Devi is not a transgender, Khushi; she is an intersex. There is a lot of difference between them. That is why she doesn't look like them. Transgender is a very broad term, among them there are many types. The person could be a Hijra – a man who is born with the male reproductive organ, but identifies himself with the female gender as he grows up; or an intersex, a person born with a sexual anatomy which does not fit into the typical definition of both a male and a female. There are also trans men – persons born with female reproductive organs who identify themselves as men.

"The term 'transsexual' is used to refer to someone who has undergone surgery to align his or her body with the gender they want to identify themselves with and 'transvestites' are those who enjoy wearing clothes of a different gender."

"This is so interesting. All said and done, I guess they are as much human as us. Different, yes. But why doesn't the world like them? I could write a book on them, there is so much the world doesn't know about them."

"That is not possible Khushi. They don't talk about themselves, at least not in India. They are a very small, closed community that is divided into seven houses, each having a Guru. I was surprised when Chandani told us her story today. I had tried speaking to Sharmila about her life once and she had refused point blank; she said that they were not allowed to speak about themselves without the permission of their Guru."

"Maa, you know so much about them."

"I have to; I have a child like them. I read this beautiful book by Andrew Solomon called *Tree of life*. It has an entire chapter on transgenders. It's an eye opener. He says 'love your child, no matter what' and that's exactly what I am trying to do.

"But they do have a tough life. They earn most of their living singing and dancing on marriages and child birth. So I really don't know if they earn enough to sustain themselves. That is why I am so keen on Devi finishing her education. I have to make sure she finds a way to earn her livelihood from something beyond dancing and singing. She already has enough to deal with; being a woman trapped inside a man's body is already very hard. I don't want her to have to struggle to make ends meet."

"Do you think you will be able to do that? I don't mean to discourage you, but it seems that the forces are working against you."

"I am trying, Khushi, let us see. I have always had Naveen by my side and now I have you. I am sure we will find a way."

The start of a revolution

☿

Naina was determined to find a way to educate and empower Devi. Meanwhile Khushi went to the kothi everyday to teach Devi. She left for Delhi the evening before Devi's exams were to start. Devi gave her papers one after the other in the principal's room. Khushi would call her after every paper to ask how she had done. The day Devi finished her papers she said to Father Peter, "Father, I have a question. May I ask?"

"Yes, my child. But quickly please. I have to go."

"If I teach my people, will you allow them to sit through the papers like you allowed me?"

Father Peter was caught completely off guard. "I don't know my child, I really don't know. But it is a very noble thought; I shall think about this."

Devi left the school ten minutes after all the students had left. Sharmila was waiting for her in the auto. There had been a transgender murder in the city a few days ago and not wanting to take a chance with Devi's safety, Chandani had put Sharmila on the job of escorting Devi again.

The next morning was a historic day for the transgenders. In a landmark judgment, the Supreme Court had created the "third gender" status for Hijras or transgenders. Earlier, they were forced to write male or female against their gender. The Supreme Court had also asked the Centre to treat transgender as socially and economically backward class. The ruling had decreed that transgenders would be allowed admission in educational institutions and given employment. The Hijras were absolutely delighted. Chandani threw a huge party that night. They invited Naina, Naveen and Srishti too.

Naina met Naveen outside the kothi. "Why didn't you get Srishti?"

"She said she was not feeling up to it."

"Okay. And what is that you are carrying in your hand? Another gift for Devi?"

"How did you know? Yes, it's a laptop."

"Thank you, Naveen. Srishti is one lucky woman to have you for her husband."

"I am the lucky one to have Devi in my life. I have a very strong feeling that she will score at least ninety percent in her boards. I am so excited that it feels like I am waiting for *my* report card." They both smiled and went inside.

The Hijras were dancing and singing loudly. They clapped and danced right through the night and also made Naveen and Naina join them.

"I am happy today, Naina. I just hope that Srishti has a baby soon," Naveen said to Naina later that night, as he drove her home.

"You both are crazy, you know that, right? She is forty now. The biological clock is ticking. Why don't you two simply go adopt a baby. Haven't you guys tried enough already?"

"She is not willing to give up. She is hopeful that she will get pregnant."

"Go make love to her tonight. She will have a baby," Naina said to Naveen as she got out of the car.

"Yes, yes!" he shouted and left.

As Naveen was driving, he thought about the Supreme Court judgment and how Devi would be able to attend regular school next year. But whether or not the students would accept her as one of them was still a question to be answered.

✗

It was peak summers in Rajasthan. The temperature had hit a scorching forty-five degrees. Devi didn't have much to do. Most of the regular kids joined some extracurricular class or the other during the summers, but Devi stayed indoors. One day, she was reading a book when Sharmila came to see her. "You are so lucky Devi; I wish I could read too."

"Why didn't you say anything before? I can teach you."

"Really? When can we start?"

"Immediately!"

Excited, Devi gave Sharmila a copy and a pencil. "How much do you remember of what you had read in class when you were in your village?"

"Not much, but let me try." Sharmila wrote the entire alphabet in Hindi and then wrote her name.

"Wow!" Devi said, as they ran upstairs to the store and found Devi's old books stacked neatly in one corner.

Chandani was out of station for some conference of all the Gurus. Nothing could happen in the kothi without her permission. But Devi had started teaching Sharmila anyway. The wedding season was over; the Hijras did not have much work except going for the celebration of new born babies. Devi had started teaching Sharmila in the mornings and evenings. Both of them had found a new direction in life. A few days later, Sanna joined them. "I want to start studying too, Devi. Will you teach me?"

Sharmila answered before Devi could. "Yes, yes. She will teach you."

Devi smiled, so they were three of them now. One by one, all of them joined in. Devi called Naveen and told him what was happening. Next day, Naveen sent a huge white board and some pens so that Devi could teach them all easily. They put the white board in the hall and Devi became their teacher.

There was one among them, Pooja, who did not join them. She repeatedly warned them that no decision had ever been taken in the kothi without Chandani's permission and that they would all be in big trouble when she found out. Devi could not see any reason why Chandani would get upset; as a matter of fact, she thought Chandani would be very happy to see Hijras studying. They would sit in groups all day and practice writing. They were like a group of nursery kids who would write the alphabets at least ten times to get them right.

When Chandani came back after a month, Pooja went to pick her up at the railway station. On the way back, she told Chandani all that had been happening at the kothi. "For the first time, something has happened in our kothi without your permission. Devi is teaching everybody."

The Hijras live in well-defined and organized communities led by a Guru. A Guru is the head of his chelas or dependants. He protects them and takes care of their daily needs, and they in return, obey him and give their earnings to him. The Hijras of India are a religious community who renounce male sexuality. Although they may use male, female or gender neutral pronouns, they usually insist on being referred to with feminine pronouns. Some Hijras undergo an initiation rite into the Hijra community called nirwaan, which refers to the removal of penis, testicles and scrotum. A Guru and his chelas usually belong to one house which is given a name. A Guru passes down his wealth to one of his senior chelas. A Guru is ideally for life; changing Gurus is mostly frowned upon. The Hijras believe that one cannot live without a Guru as a child cannot live without his mother. If any kind of a dispute arises within the house, the Guru resolves it. The Gurus of different houses of the same city form a council of the elders called a Jamat. This group takes all the important decisions as and when required. When a Hijra dies, it is the members of her house who arrange the funeral. In addition to the regional groupings of Hijras, there is also a loose national organization, which mainly meets on the anniversary of the death of an important Hijra Guru.

Everyone came to pay their respects to Chandani as she entered the house and Devi excitedly came forward to tell Chandani her big secret.

"Mom, guess what? I am teaching everyone here; everyone will be educated."

Chandani was furious. "Couldn't you have taken my permission? Who gave you the authority to start teaching them? This is my kothi and you are but a fourteen-year-old kid. Don't you dare overstep your boundaries," she thundered.

Devi was absolutely taken aback and started crying. "But I don't understand. I thought you would be proud of me. Education can change our lives. Even the court has allowed the Hijras to seek admission in schools now. Then why are you stopping me?"

"You don't teach me what I should do and what I shouldn't. They are my people and I know what's best for them. Even if they go to a school, the world will not accept them. You will show them false dreams and spoil all their conditioning, as a result of which, they will become even more miserable."

"But mom, they are not going to any school. I am teaching them in our world here."

"I said no! Now there will be no more discussion on this."

Devi was absolutely shocked. There was pin drop silence outside, as they had all huddled together to hear the argument. She called Naveen and asked him to send someone to collect the board and the pens. Naveen, who never got scared of anything, came to meet Chandani and had an hour long discussion with her. As he stepped out of her room, he showed thumbs up to all of them. They all blessed him. He hugged Devi and told her to carry on her good work. The classes started once again, and this time, Pooja joined them too.

As Naveen was driving back home, he got a call from Srishti. Naveen listened to the phone before yelling into the phone. "WHAT? I don't believe this. I am coming home immediately." Naveen parked his car in the driveway and ran to their room. Srishti hugged him and said, "I am pregnant." He held her tight as both of them shed tears of happiness.

"Have you told anybody yet?"

"No!"

"Let's go to a gynaecologist first and see what she has to say."

Naveen and Srishti held hands as they drove to the Santokba Durlabhji Memorial Hospital. Dr Megha, who knew Naveen well, ran some tests on Srishti and confirmed that she was pregnant.

Naveen was delighted. They first went to the Ganesh Temple at Moti Doongri to thank the lord and then he took Srishti to Chandani. Naveen and Srishti touched her feet and announced her pregnancy. Naveen told her that the impossible had happened, all thanks to the blessings of the Hijras. Srishti told Chandni that she wanted to thank Sharmila more than anybody else, as she was the one who had asked everyone to bless her. Chandani called for Sharmila and Shristi touched her feet. Sharmila smiled and blessed her once again.

Naveen called Naina and almost shouted into the phone, "Srishti is pregnant!"

"Oh God! Congratulations! I can't believe that this is finally happening for you guys."

Srishti smiled as they talked. Naveen and Naina shared an amazing bond. It made Srishti a little jealous at times, but there was nothing she could do about it, so she learnt to ignore it.

Srishti was lost in her own thoughts as Naveen drove her back home. Some Hijras were said to have spiritual powers and were considered sacred. Maybe Naveen is right. Maybe, I am pregnant today because of their blessings, she thought.

The results of the tenth standard board examination were announced the next morning. Naveen opened the CBSE website and typed Devi's roll number. She had scored a total of ninety percent marks. Naveen was so happy that he started jumping in his cabin.

He messaged Naina who was in Bali for a family holiday.

Madam, we have scored a 90 % in our 10th boards.

She replied sending him emoticons, two hugs and a big smile.

Excited, Naveen drove up to Devi's house with one big bucket of her favourite chocolate ice-cream. Devi hugged him as he entered. The Hijras were jubilant; they were dancing and singing badhai-congratulatory songs already. Chandani was quietly sitting in one corner. Naveen walked up to her.

"What happened?"

"Just fever as always." She sighed.

"You really need to take care of yourself."

"Don't worry Naveen, it will go. It's mild fever. Comes and goes."

"I know it's mild, but it means your immunity is low."

"Please forget about me. I am getting old. I am one proud mother today. I have only you to thank."

"Oh! Come on. We have all done our bit."

They both sat and watched everyone dance.

The arrival of Ameena

☿

It was time for the schools to reopen and Naveen went to school to talk to Father Peter about Devi's schooling. Now that it was legal, he wanted Devi to attend regular school. Father Peter told Naveen that he had no problems with that. Naveen was very happy and called Devi to tell her the news, but Devi refused to go to regular school. She said she would never be comfortable with the other students and wanted to let everything carry on the way it was. But it was getting difficult for Naina and Naveen to teach her now. It had been almost nineteen years since they had left college and a lot had changed since then. After a lot of discussion, Devi finally agreed to use the webcams once again. The principal already had cameras installed all over the school for the purpose of security, so they decided that she could sit in an isolated room and attend all the classes through her laptop. And the teachers could be asked to give her a one-on-one class for half an hour twice a week.

Devi soon got busy with classes and her home work and assignments. She would come home after school and teach the rest of the gang who would be eagerly waiting for her. They were all beginning to enjoy every minute of studying. Devi's hands were full, but she was enjoying herself thoroughly.

Khushi was in her second year of college and was happy with Pranay. They had both decided to go to the US for their post-graduation and had started doing their research on the courses available.

Kavish was also growing up fast; he was in the eighth standard now. Naina was happy with her life; all her kids were happy and settled for now. The only one thing that kept bothering her was Devi's future. She wanted to somehow make sure that Devi found a way to earn decent money. But the child had zero exposure. She had never even stepped out of Jaipur. What would she do in life?

In the newspaper the next day, there was a half page advertisement for IIM Ahmedabad. They too had opened their doors to the transgenders. They had allowed the third gender to apply for the upcoming joint entrance examinations. Other leading institutes like MNIT and NID were also planning to let transgenders apply for the next session's examinations as their admission process for the current year was already over.

But this was just a trickle in the ocean and it would be a long time before anybody could apply for admission to these institutes; the Hijras were not even educated up to the primary level. But Devi was; maybe she would be able to get through and that thought made Naina smile.

Naina was considerably free now and was getting quite bored with life. One day she called Naveen. "How is Srishti doing?"

"She is nice and pregnant, doing just fine."

"That's cute. Listen, do you know if there is an age bar to join a post-graduation course in Economics?"

"I don't think so. But you should go to the university and check, or just visit their website. You'll find everything you need there."

"Thank you so much." She felt like an idiot. Why did it not strike her to simply go online and check. She found out that there was no age bar for post-graduation courses; in fact, the admissions for the current academic year were still open. She quickly searched through her shelves for her documents and applied for the course.

Naveen was doing very well for himself by now. He had been doing a lot of work for the government. He and his team were handling the media campaign for the Rajasthan wing of the BJP.

Even Manish's company was growing very fast. While they had no major innovation in the past few years, but his biggest strength was the service they gave to their clients.

Sometime in March, while Devi was preparing for her eleventh standard exams, a strange guest arrived in their house. Her name was Ameena, and she had come from Lucknow. She was suffering from depression and did not talk to anybody. She had a huge masculine body, and was quite fat. She could always be found sitting in some corner of the hall and would often start crying. She had been sent to Jaipur because her Guru had hoped that the change may help her get better. All the members of the kothi got so scared of the way she was, that they did not talk to her much. It was only when they sat together for the meals that one of them went and fetched her. No one knew what her story was; some said that she could never come to terms with the fact that she was a transgender while the others said that her family threw her out and that is why she got depressed. Chandani had given special instructions to everyone to be kind to her, but everybody just stayed away from her. Some secretly hoped that she would leave as soon as possible; they didn't like having this depressed soul around the happy, lively kothi.

Devi continued to teach the Hijras. Some of them were picking up very fast and some were slightly slow. One day, while Devi was teaching, the doorbell rang. A gentleman had arrived, requesting them to attend his son's wedding. He left thirty-five plain pink odhnis with a golden border for each one of them. Sharmila put the packet on the side of the room and hurriedly re-joined the class.

Ameena had been sitting quietly all this time; she pulled the packet towards herself and removed one odhni from it. She got up and went to the end of the hall, opened her suitcase and started looking for something inside it. She removed one big box of thick colorful threads and a thick needle. She sat down in one corner and quietly started doing embroidery on the odhni. She had embroidered one small flower on the corner with a blue thread. She looked at it and smiled. After Devi finished teaching them, they put the board aside and put on the television. Devi was sitting on the floor at the end of the hall near Ameena; she did not enjoy watching serials. She noticed the beautifully embroidered corner of the dupatta. "Wow!" she said. Ameena just looked up and started embroidering again. Ameena sat in some corner of the kothi and embroidered the odhni, little by little, all day long.

Srishti's water bag burst one night. Naveen rushed her to the hospital where she gave birth to a baby girl. Naveen was delighted and checked on the baby at least twenty times a day. Devi came with Chandani to bless the baby. Naveen's mother got up, touched Chandani's feet and asked for her blessings.

Naveen had told his entire family that Srishti had conceived only because the Hijras had blessed them. Naina was there too; she had got Naveen a huge bouquet of flowers and a lot of gifts for the baby. She marvelled at the attitude of Naveen's family towards the Hijras, as compared to that of hers.

Devi's eleventh standard results were out. She had scored an astounding ninety-three percent. Khushi and Pranay were busy planning their post-graduation in the US. The Kapoors were happy but Mithila ji was apprehensive about sending Khushi with Pranay without getting them married first. She spoke to Manish about her concerns when he came home one evening. Manish spoke to Nikhil and the Kapoors were invited home for dinner to discuss the matter.

Naina and her maids cleaned the house and made an elaborate dinner for the Kapoors. The two families decided that Khushi and Pranay should be married before leaving for the States. Khushi and Pranay were not too happy with the whole idea, but succumbed to family pressure.

Naveen and Srishti got busy with the new born baby, Devi with her twelfth standard and Naina with the preparations for the wedding.

Time passed quickly and the big day arrived. Khushi had come back to Jaipur fifteen days before the wedding. She went to meet Devi and told her about the wedding. Devi hugged and congratulated her. Khushi had brought a plain gold finger ring and a beautiful anarkali suit for Devi. Khushi choked with emotion when Devi wrapped her arms around her. Devi would not be able to attend the wedding and Khushi felt terrible about it.

As the Malhotras sang and danced at the wedding, Devi sat in her room with the laptop, trying to understand how to start an e-commerce website.

That night, the Malhotras bid farewell to their daughter. Khushi Malhotra had become Khushi Kapoor. After Khushi left, Naina and Manish were alone in their room. Exhausted, Naina was slowly removing all the jewellery and make up, when for the first time in years, Manish asked about Devi. "Khushi told me that Devi is pretty and very nice. Does she look like you?"

Naina, upset about Devi not being able to attend the wedding, snapped at him. "How is it any of your business, Mr Malhotra?"

✗

Ameena, after about thirty days of non-stop embroidery, had made a stunning and unique odhni. Half of it had Lucknowi chicken embroidery, and the other half, Kashmiri. The two patterns fused together and the overall effect was beautiful. The Hijras were amazed to see the odhni.

The next day, Chandani bought a big box of colourful threads and gifted it to Ameena, who then started doing the embroidery on another odhni.

Time flew by and Devi took her twelfth standard board exams. She had opted for Science and Maths on Naveen's insistence in the eleventh standard. She did nothing but study the whole day long. She was the only one in school who did not take any extra tuition in the evening. She could not afford it, but Father Peter was very kind. Each time she got stuck somewhere, he would either teach her himself or send a teacher to help her. She was a big girl now and did not like the idea of asking Naveen or Naina for anything extra.

Soon Devi's results were announced. She had scored a ninety-four percent this year. Everybody was happy. But Naina was starting to get worried again. *Now what?* she thought. Naveen thought she was crazy when she confided her fears in him. Devi was a brilliant child with amazing scores. She could get admission anywhere she liked. No college could refuse her. But Naina knew that it would not be half as easy as Naveen made it sound.

The night Devi's results were announced, Chandani summoned her to her room. "You are a big girl now, Devi, and I want you to start earning. You must go out with the group now and do your duties towards the kothi."

Devi was speechless. She had wanted to join college and complete her education. Understanding her concern, Chandani continued, "You can study; I am not stopping you. But you must also earn."

Devi did not reply. She had never stepped out with the Hijras for work; she loved to sing and dance, but was horrified at the thought of singing and dancing outside people's houses. She remembered what Naina had said to her once.

You are made for bigger things, Devi. Remember that always.

Trans Color

⚦

Naina and Naveen were both doing their research about various colleges. Naveen wanted to send her to engineering colleges and Naina wanted to send her to business management institutes. They had both not spoken about it to each other yet and what was worse was that they had not spoken to Devi about it.

Naina had downloaded a whole lot of admission forms, but they never had an option for the third gender. Naina had sent requests for her admission to various institutes across the country with a photo copy of her mark sheet and a request letter mentioning her gender status. Naveen had done the same.

Naina was very keen on sending Devi to Christ College in Bangalore. It was run by Christian missionaries and had a Bachelor's course in business administration too. She hoped that Father Peter could put in a word of recommendation for Devi and that she would be happy and safe there. She was very apprehensive about sending her anywhere else.

Naveen hurriedly came to Devi one day with a whole lot of papers in his hands. He gave Devi a pen and asked her to sign them. "At least tell me what I am signing?"

"It's an admission form; for engineering in Chennai."

"But who will employ me once I finish my engineering?"

"What's wrong with you Devi? Once you have an engineering degree, why wouldn't anyone employ you?"

"I am not going anywhere, dad. I will join Xavier's College here in Jaipur."

"Why didn't you tell me this earlier? And have you lost your mind? How can you give up an opportunity like that?"

"It is only the admission form. I haven't got admission yet."

"But you will. I have spoken to the director and he has agreed. In fact, no one can say no to you now; it is legal."

"But I do not want to go."

"Give me one good reason why?"

"Dad, you and I are different; you do not understand everything about my life, so let us not talk about it."

"At least try to make me understand, Devi. I am your father."

"I am scared of not being accepted, of being made fun of, of being lonely."

"But you have to learn to face all this. How long will you keep running away from everything? When you were younger, we had no other option but to send you to St. Xavier's. But now, the whole world is open to you. You must step out of your cocoon to get exposure and grow as a person."

"I can go to the Xavier's College here."

"Right now, Xavier's College is just a building; it does not even have a proper campus yet. There is no comparison between the Chennai College of Engineering and Xavier's. How will you learn about new things Devi? When will you see the world?"

"I don't belong to your world. Why don't you understand that? I just can't relate to anyone there."

"So what am I supposed to do? Open a college for transgenders? I don't have that kind of money."

"See, I told you. You will never understand. I don't want to become an engineer."

"Why didn't you say anything earlier? I would have not made all this effort then."

"You did not ask me!"

Naveen kept quiet. He really hadn't bothered to ask her.

"Remember you once told me that in Jaipur there were a lot of business families whose kids studied in Jaipur itself and started working right after school. They learnt their subject so well that they are better than any Ph.D. holders in their subject."

"Yes, I did. But they are kids from business families, mostly jewellers. They learn as they work, and yes, they are masters at their work. You are missing a point here. First, you don't belong to a business family, so you can't learn like them. And second, those people travel abroad very often for work and get their exposure from there."

"I could learn from you, dad."

"What do you know about advertising? Come on, tell me!"

"I don't know anything, but you can teach me."

"Do you like advertising? It's a different world. It requires a different skill set which I learnt when I went to college."

"I hope you understand that I don't belong to your world."

"I am losing my mind Devi. So before I get angry, tell me what is it that you want to do and how do you intend to earn your living."

"I have a plan Dad, and if you help me, you and I can work it out."

She went to her room and got her laptop. She had an entire presentation ready. "But first, can we call both my moms?"

"Call Chandani. But Nania will take at least twenty minutes to reach here. I can't wait for that long. I will tell her everything later."

At that moment, Naina walked in. "Look who is here?"

Naveen looked at her and said, "Shut up and sit down Naina. I have exactly fifteen minutes."

Devi started with her presentation. "First, I am not going anywhere outside Jaipur. I am absolutely sure about it. Second, I will take up a course in Business Management at Xavier's. I have spoken to Father Peter about it, continuing to study through webcams as before. Third, I want to start an e-commerce website called *Trans Color*."

She turned her laptop towards them and showed a picture of the beautifully embroidered red dupatta. It had *Trans Color* written in yellow over a light blue background.

Naveen smiled and looked at Naina, absolutely amazed.

"It will have an in-built payment gateway where you can make payments through your credit card and software that will generate an invoice automatically once the payment is reflected in our account."

"And what will we sell?"

Devi brought out the beautifully embroidered cotton odhni and showed it to all of them!

Naina held it in her hand and couldn't help gasping. "Devi, this is stunning! This is the most intricate handiwork I have ever seen. Who is the designer?"

"Our very own Ameena!"

"What about the finances?" Naveen asked.

"That I still have to figure out."

"Get me a plan and if I like it, you can stay. If I don't, you will go to Chennai." Naveen got up. His arm brushed against Chandani's. He touched her forehead. "You have fever again?" he said surprised

Chandani nodded and Naveen said more sternly, "I really think you need to see a doctor."

"I am just fine."

"You are not. Please see a doctor." He turned towards Naina and Devi, "Take care all of you."

Naveen left, leaving Naina and Devi to their thoughts.

"So tell me, how will Ameena alone take care of all the production? How long does it take to make one odhni?" Naina asked Devi.

"I haven't thought of that. It takes almost thirty days to finish one."

Chandani had listening quietly all this while, and piped up. "From tomorrow, we will ask Ameena to teach all of us. That way we can produce thirty-four pieces each month."

"And no odhnis please; just make simple two-and-a-half metre dupattas, small stoles and scarves. You should do this on georgettes, silks and chiffons," Naina suggested.

After a while, Naina got up to leave. Devi walked her to the door. "So, what do you think Mom?"

"I am so proud of you Devi." She hugged her and started crying. "But you better get to work. Take proper classes for all your people. Are they ready to take their first standard exams?"

"Most of them are. I still have one month to go before the new session starts. I have already spoken to Father Peter. He even offered to have teachers come and teach if there are enough of us. We are thirty-four; I think I can manage to convince him."

"Gear up, my girl. You have a lot of work to do. Make a proper time table! Take classes in the morning and after lunch. In the evenings, let them all learn how to do embroidery. Don't worry about the finances. We will get you a loan once the company is registered, and till then, you have your mom. I will send cotton dupattas and thread for them to practice on tomorrow."

"No mom, chill! Ameena has barely completed three odhnis. We still have more than thirty of them left. They will be enough for us to practice on."

"Then I will send the threads for you to use."

Devi hugged her once again. "Mom, please don't send me to Chennai."

"You work on your business plan and if you get stuck, just call me. I will handle Naveen. By the way, who taught you to make a business plan?"

"Honestly, I know nothing about it. I just read about it on the internet."

"Then just make rough notes and read whatever you can lay your hands on. Tomorrow you and I will make a business plan."

"Bye mom and thank you so much!"

Devi ran to Chandani's room and hugged her. She had already rounded up everyone and told them to start learning embroidery from Ameena.

Ameena still did not speak to anyone, but would now smile more often, and each time she smiled, the Hijras clapped as a rule.

Naina was so happy that she wanted to dance! She couldn't believe that Devi would soon be financially independent. She had spent days worrying about Devi. She would get nightmares about Devi dancing on the streets and people pelting her with stones.

She called Khushi that night. "Devi is starting her own company, Khushi. I am so excited."

"That's great news, mom. I have good news too. I got admission into the Bentley University in the US and so did Pranay. My dream has come true."

"Why don't you call up Devi and tell her that. She will feel nice."

"Maa, what should I tell her? That here I am in the US and getting the best education in the world, married to the man I love and you have pretty much got nothing. How do you think she would feel about it? I feel so guilty. Moreover, right now I am very busy, adjusting to a new marriage, new mumma papa, a new country and a new husband."

"A new husband?"

"Oh! You know what I mean."

"Do both of you talk much otherwise or not?"

"You mean Devi and me? I do, once in a while, but not much. We exchange a few mails too. I just don't know what to say to her. Moreover, our lives are so different, I can barely relate to her.

"The injustice that life has meted upon her is her biggest sore spot and I feel if I tell her about my life, I will only rub salt on her wounds instead of trying and putting some medicine on them so that they can heal."

"It's all in your mind Khushi. Your love and acceptance would mean the world to her."

"So I am there for her. Right? And I definitely accept her as my own and she knows that. She calls me didi. I address her as my little sister. But you must understand that I hardly know her and I have hardly spent any time with her. It's kind of difficult to bond with her suddenly. I think let's not push this relationship. She and me will connect and bond over a period of time. Blood is always thicker than water."

"Alright, you take care."

"You too, maa."

The phone started ringing as soon as she hung up. It was Chandani.

"I feel so blessed today that we have Devi. I am so proud that she is planning to open her own business. If it works out, it will transform our lives forever."

Naina smiled and said, "Please don't say if, everything will work out. I am sure about it."

"Our Devi really is a goddess, Naina. I am glad you named her Devi."

"I named her Devi because I liked the name. My thoughts never went beyond that. You take care, will see you tomorrow."

"I am so excited. Good night."

"Good night," said Naina.

Naina slept a very happy woman that night. Kavish was in the ninth standard now, doing well. She was happy going back to college. Life was on a roll.

That night she checked her bank account for the balance she had. She was not too happy with what she found. There wasn't much, but it would be enough for Devi to start. But if she gave this away, she would have no savings left. Naina remembered her father who had always said, "I don't want you to touch this money unless it's an emergency."

Naveen too was checking his accounts! Naveen and Naina were very much alike. Giving came easily to them. They were together right through college, but surprisingly. Love never blossomed between them. Or did it? Hidden somewhere in the deeper recesses of their hearts, which they never understood, or maybe preferred to keep under wraps.

The making of Trans Color

Early next morning, Devi called Naina. "Mom, I need your help. I have come up with some figures, but I don't know how to put it on paper. And if I have nothing to show by the time Dad calls, he will send me to Chennai. I really don't want to go."

Naina looked at the watch. It was 6 in the morning. It looked like Devi had stayed up all night thinking about this.

"Mom, are you there?"

"Yes, don't worry Devi. Naveen will not send you to Chennai. I will come and help you figure out the details. Does 11.00 a.m. work for you?"

"Yes. I'll see you then."

Naina felt bad for Devi. Even after all this education, she was so low on confidence. Even the idea of going to Chennai on her own was giving her jitters, and Khushi on the other hand, was desperately looking forward to going away to the States.

"I just have to work on her confidence," thought Naina.

Naina and Devi sat together and first created a list of everything they needed to start.

- A website and a website developer
- A payment gateway on the website
- Marketing strategy for the website
- The name of the company
- The company logo
- Pictures of the products
- A good low cost supplier for georgette, chiffon and silk
- Company registration
- A bank loan
- Product cost
- Selling price
- Research about the rules of taxation
- Visiting cards for Devi as director of *Trans Color*

Devi stared at the list in disbelief; she could not believe that so much work went behind starting a small website.

"Dad can be our brand consultant. We will hopefully not have to pay him. Let's go see him now with everything we've got," said Devi.

Both of them laughed as they got up to gather their material and go to Naveen's office. Naveen was busy when they reached and they were asked to wait for half an hour.

"Lesson number one: Always take an appointment before visiting somebody," Naina told Devi. She taught Devi how to send an e-mail requesting an appointment while they waited for Naveen in the visitors' lounge.

Devi quickly sent an e-mail to Naveen requesting an appointment with him. When Naveen saw the email on his phone, he smiled and excused himself from his meeting.

"You guys are crazy. You don't need to request an appointment with me. Now come with me."

"See, it worked," Naina whispered to Devi as they entered Naveen's office.

"So, what brings you two lovely ladies to my office?" Naveen asked them. Devi looked up at Naina expectantly.

"It's your company Devi, and your idea. You should do the talking."

Devi collected her thoughts, remembered everything that she had discussed with Naina and then started to speak. "Dad, I need a logo, visiting cards, a letter head and envelopes – which look really good but are low on cost."

"And what is the name of your company Devi?"

"*Trans Color.*"

"Devi, all this is great. But you still don't know the first thing about starting a business. Please go and look up on it, read as much as you can. There are thousands of videos and tutorials on business management on YouTube. It's not half as easy as it sounds."

"Alright dad," she said, absolutely disappointed.

"You don't have to get disappointed. The world is your sea; you just have to learn to swim. From today, I am your brand consultant. But first, you need to get your company registered, open a bank account and then come back to me with the details."

"And how does one do that?"

"Don't worry; I will help you with everything. But first, I want you to do your research. If you need to understand anything, just call anytime of the day."

"Till then, at least get her visiting cards designed for her," Naina said.

"Yes, I will get onto that. You shall have the quotation in your inbox within the hour. Sign it and put your company seal confirming your approval. My team will start working on your brand development as soon as I have your approval on the prices. And, just for you, I shall give a forty percent discount on my usual rates."

Devi stared at Naveen. She didn't know how to answer. Bidding farewell, they got up and left from the office.

"What happened Devi?" Naina asked, seeing tears flowing down Devi's face.

"Mom, dad is asking me to pay, but I don't have a single penny."

"Please don't worry Devi. I and Naveen are both giving you a loan of two lakhs each; and four lakhs is more than what you require as an initial investment."

Devi looked at Naina in surprise, "You are giving me a loan?"

"Yes, a business loan."

Devi took a deep breath and sounding absolutely bitter, she asked, "At what rate of interest?"

"The same as what a bank would charge you."

Devi did not say another word till Naina pulled up in front of Chandani's house. "Bye!" she said and got off.

Naveen rounded up his entire team minutes after they left. "I want you to develop the best brand possible for this company called *Trans Color*. Give me four options for everything. Don't worry about the costs; the details are in this file. I will settle for nothing but the best."

✕

Devi found Chandani sitting on the cot in her room. She just hugged her and wept. "They would never have done the same to Khushi or Rhea," she wailed.

"You know, it is sad Devi that you have still not learnt to trust your parents. I am sure they have their reasons in doing all this. We should never judge someone solely on what they say. We should try to understand their intention behind it. Now go to your room and start working, we have a lot to do!"

Devi wiped her tears and turned around to leave. "By the way, who is Rhea?" Chandani asked her. Devi told her she was Naveen's daughter and left the room.

She got something to eat and opened up her laptop. She already had an e-mail from Naveen's office in her inbox. Devi examined the rates, but she had never seen a quotation before in her life. She opened the excel sheet which Naina had asked her to make, and put the details of the company and the quotation on it.

She then ran a Google search on registering a company. She carefully went through the information and noted down everything she needed to do. The biggest challenge would be to go to a government organization and get the registration done. She went to Sharmila and asked her what she should do. Sharmila asked her to not worry at all as she knew somebody in the ROC (Registrars of Companies) office who could help them.

Next day, a man by the name of Hanif Khan came to their kothi. Sharmila, who was expecting him, ushered him in as soon as he rang the bell.

He told them that it would be difficult because all the forms have only male or female options for the proprietor or the partners. There are no options for the other sexes. He also said that they would have to pay him two thousand rupees if he manages to get the company registered.

"But the cost of registration is only five hundred rupees," said Devi from behind.

Hanif frowned. "Yes, the cost of registration is five hundred rupees, which will have to be paid apart from the two thousand rupees. It is my fees for getting your work done."

Sharmila paid him five hundred rupees and told him that he will get the rest once the registration was done.

"Get a seal made for your company," he said, clutching the five hundred rupees note and left.

"What is this seal now?" Devi asked Sharmila. "Please see if you can find someone who can get this done."

Sharmila was not perturbed; Devi watched her as she dialled number after number. "*Seal banwani hai!...han seal!*" She was yelling on the phone. Sharmila's networking had always amazed Devi. She seemed to know everybody.

A fortnight passed and Hanif had still not gotten back to them. Sharmila called him to get an update. He told them that there were no forms which give an option for the third gender and that he needed more time. Sharmila couldn't understand the problem as the third gender had been legalized.

Naina talked to Naveen – who was always short on time – about going to the bank to get the accounts opened. She knew he'd have to sign a few papers as Devi was a minor. Naveen asked Devi to meet him at the bank the next morning with her Aadhaar card to get an account opened. "We will open a co-operative, dad. We will all be the owners," Devi told Naveen when all thirty-five of them met him at the bank.

"Do they all have Aadhaar cards?" Naveen asked Naina.

"Some of them do."

"The bank won't let them open their bank accounts without any identity cards."

"Most of them have their driving licence. Let's just go in and see how it goes."

Meanwhile, college started and Devi also had to attend her lectures through the webcam.

Another two months passed before the company was finally registered. Sharmila hugged Hanif with joy when he came with the papers. When Devi called Naveen to tell him the good news, he told her to come and see him the next afternoon and bring Naina along.

When Devi and Naina reached Naveen's office the next afternoon, he showed them designs for the visiting card, the envelope and the letter head one by one. They were all very beautifully done. Everything was appealing and classy. Overjoyed, Devi jumped up and hugged Naveen.

"Now we need a website," he said pulling himself away from her strong arms.

Naina immediately called her friend Sandeep and said, "I need an appointment; I am sending someone very special to you."

The next morning, Naina drove Devi to Sandeep's office. She told her to go inside alone, saying that she couldn't hold her hand forever. Devi took a deep breath and stepped out of the car. As she walked into the office, she saw three rows of people working on their laptops. She walked up to the man sitting right in front and gave him her visiting card with both hands as Naina had taught her to. Naina had specially made her wear a long cobalt-blue skirt with a white top and a pair of white sandals. First impression is always the last impression," Naina had said before driving to Sandeep's office.

Devi was also carrying a note pad in which Naina had made her list of all the questions that she should ask and on another page, all the information he would want. "One should always be prepared for a meeting Devi," Naina had explained.

Two minutes later, she was told that Mr Sandeep was expecting her. Sandeep got up to greet her as she entered his office. He shook hands with Devi and asked her to take a seat.

"Naina tells me you want to get a website made. Tell me all about it," he said.

Devi told him everything; she had put down all the information on a paper so she wouldn't miss something out. He then explained to her all that he required from her. He was also kind enough to explain all that was involved in developing and marketing a website.

He called someone from his office and instructed them to send her a quotation for the services. They shook hands once again before Devi left.

Naina was waiting for Devi outside. She smiled as Devi sat down in the car and asked her how the meeting went. "The meeting went well. Sandeep said he will make the website for us and will be sending a quote shortly."

"See, I told you everything will work out. Now we just need one more quote, so we can compare the rates. We can't place the order without proper research. So I am taking you to another website developer. Talk to him and ask for a quotation."

"Yes! Yes! Let's go!"

Naina smiled at her enthusiasm.

Achievement

☿

Devi had become a very busy girl. Naina was by her side throughout and taught her everything she knew about running a business. She would talk to Naveen at the end of each day and get his inputs as well. Naina was also learning with each passing day and she passed everything she learnt from Naveen to Devi.

After school, Devi ran from one meeting to the other, to the website developer for further discussion and to Naveen with the samples for his inputs. Rest of her time would be spent either in studying or teaching the rest of the transgenders who would wait eagerly for their evening classes. The transgenders sat all over the kothi doing embroidery. Ameena would move from one person to the other, dishing out instructions and advice about the color of the thread and the patterns. She had started speaking, but only when absolutely needed. She was the busiest of them all. Devi had told her very clearly that she wanted thirty pieces ready by the end of the month.

Slowly the website had also started taking shape. The first time it was uploaded, Devi showed it to everyone. They had all huddled together and stared at the laptop screen. Once the images appeared, they all clapped loudly!

The community had a new goal; they held hands and moved towards it. Time was ticking and Devi was starting to get worried. She would soon have to pay the interest on her loan and there was still so much left to do. The payment gateway was still to be configured. The website had to be marketed and promoted before they could launch it and it wasn't even ready yet.

Then one evening Naveen called and said that the designs were getting repetitive. He needed some variety. Devi was perplexed. They only knew two types of embroidery – Kashmiri and Lucknowi. A puzzled Devi called Naina for advice. "Dad says he wants some more variety. How are we supposed to get variety now?"

"Do you guys know someone in Gujarat?"

"Of course! Why didn't I think about this earlier? There are so many of our community in Gujarat. Let me find out. Thanks mom."

Sharmila was put on the job of finding somebody in Gujarat who could come and teach them some embroidery. After about two months, everything was in order. The designs were ready, the website was up and running, the payment gateway was sorted. Now, all they needed were orders.

Devi checked every day, sometimes multiple times a day. But there was nothing. Fifteen days later, they received their first order. Devi got an alert on her phone from the bank about a transfer from some Shaista Ali in Dubai. She was in class at that time and couldn't wait to go home and check the website for the order details. She opened up her laptop as soon as she reached home and there she saw the order that was waiting for her in blue. She quickly called everyone and told them the news. They hugged each other in jubilation as Ameena wept and smiled through her tears.

In the first month, they had only ten orders and the next month, twenty. Devi had divided everybody's responsibilities. Sharmila, being the smartest took care of the logistics and the bank affairs. Ameena was their designer and Salma, their production head. They also had a purchase head Savitri, who managed the purchase of the georgette, threads, needles and frames. She also acted as the chief coordinator between them and the supplier from Gujarat. Devi took care of all administration. Pooja was their head chef (food was important), and Chandini was the CEO.

Naveen introduced the bright chiffon dupattas with the four-inch Gujarati borders after the first fifty dupattas were shipped. He had priced them at 110 dollars each. "I don't want any repeats in designs. No more than two pieces should look alike. Make them up-market and make them exclusive."

One day Naina walked in said, "Devi, I hope you have filed your returns to the sales tax department." Devi looked at her confused.

"Who is your accountant?" Naina asked.

Devi said, "Nobody."

"Then hire one! You will need him."

Next day, Naveen had sent his accountant to Devi who gave her a lecture on book-keeping. They appointed a part-time accountant on his recommendation, who would come in once a week and make all the entries on the computer.

Orders started pouring in from across the world. Their orders soon overshot their stock and Devi started panicking. Naveen put a delivery time of ten days after the receipt of payment against each picture. Devi was learning every day; every single day brought with itself new problems and new solutions. Within a year, they started receiving over fifty orders per month.

The year they formed the company, the Hijras skipped their annual trip to Koovagam for the festival. They went to the Gujarat festival instead. It saved commuting time and they could also discuss business with their associates there.

Within two years of going online, *Trans Color* had associations with Hijras in three different states. The kothi at Haji colony had become more of an office than a home. Three office desks had been set up in the hall, equipped with laptops, scanners, printers and other office supplies. Behind the desks was a huge old wooden cupboard which they had pulled out of one of the rooms and cleaned. The temple of Lord Aravan was still there, but with very little open space left in front. They would start their morning with the pooja, after which Devi would leave for college and they would all settle down to do some embroidery. Devi would be back by noon and take two hours of classes for the Hijras which would end with a quick business discussion. The Hijras had studied enough to be at par with a third standard child. Sharmila had also learned to use the laptop. The third laptop was for Parvati and the part-time accountant who came in from time to time. Parvati had also learnt to use Excel sheets for her costing.

They contacted DHL Express for international express mailing and signed a corporate agreement with them. The Hijras didn't go to anybody. They would ask people to come to them if they wanted business, and they did.

Naina was finally at peace. One day she told Devi that she was going to Tirupati to get her hair tonsured.

"Why?" Devi asked.

Naina told her that she had vowed that the day her daughter Devi became financially independent, she will get her hair tonsured. Devi said, "Mom, I still need you. I always will!" Chandani overheard their conversation and expressed her wish to go with Naina.

"Don't worry about me, I will be just fine. You don't need to accompany me, Chandani."

"I am not going for you, I am going for Devi. I am her mother too."

Naina got train tickets done for both of them. Manish was surprised by this sudden development, but he knew he couldn't argue about certain things with Naina. She will do what she wanted to, especially when it came to Devi. So he did not even try to dissuade her from going.

The day Naina and Chandni left for Tirupati, Devi received a letter from the Export cell of the Government of India that *Trans Color* had been chosen for the award of the best exporter for the year. The award was to be given away at the Birla Auditorium in a small ceremony by Mr Chetan Bishnoi, the Minister for Small Scale Industries.

Devi was delighted. The Hijras stopped work, pushed the chairs and tables in a corner and danced like they had never danced before. The accountant was all smiles and joined them too.

Devi called Naveen, "Dad, you are getting an award!" She told him about the letter. Naveen was ecstatic.

"I don't believe this! Wow! That is amazing news, Devi."

"Please go and collect the award, Dad. It's on the 30th."

"Devi, it's not my award. This is your achievement and you will go to receive it personally."

Devi disconnected the line and joined in the dancing once again.

Meanwhile, Naina and Chandani got their hair tonsured. Chandani had insisted on it saying she was Devi's mother too.

The award

☿

It was the 30th of April. The hall at Birla Auditorium was filled to capacity. Cars came in one after the other as government officials and political big wigs entered the hall. At about 6, there was commotion outside. Security guards with their walkie talkies rushed outside. A huge group of Hijras had gathered there and wanted to get in.

"What is it that you want?" the head of security, Deepak Chauhan asked them.

Devi showed him the invitation letter from the government.

"Who is Devi Sharma?" he asked after inspecting the letter.

"That's me," Devi said, showing him a visiting card.

"You can step in. The rest need to leave now," said Deepak.

"Either we all go in or no one does!"

"Let me check," he said, and disappeared inside the hall.

All of them were dressed in plain saris with heavily embroidered blouses, one of their new line of products. The blouses were yet to go online. They had wanted to flaunt it before the world saw it. Devi, also dressed in a sari, looked beautiful as ever. Naina had gifted her a set of solitaire earrings which adorned her ears.

Naveen's car pulled up in front of the hall as they waited. He stepped inside and created a mini-ruckus, "Why are you stopping them? Who is going to receive the award?"

Within five minutes they were all ushered in and shown to comfortable seats on the first floor hall. "Are you sure you want to do this?" Devi asked Naina as she came and sat next to her. Naina just nodded in agreement.

The chief guest arrived and the evening began with the lamp lighting ceremony. The minister was garlanded and the emcee thanked him for his presence. Speeches were made and finally the award ceremony began. Naina held her hand as Devi shifted nervously on her seat. Soon it was time for Devi's award.

"And the award for the Best Exporter goes to Trans Color! May I call upon Devi sharma to receive the award on behalf of the Trans Color team?" Devi got up from her chair and walked down the stairs with Sharmila. She took a deep breath, looked at Sharmila and together they walked down the red carpet. The crowd looked at them, shocked. There was complete silence in the hall. Most people kept looking over their shoulders for Devi Sharma. As Devi walked onto the stage, the minister looked at her completely baffled, but then a huge smile appeared on his face.

He presented the award to her and took the mike. "Aren't you going to clap for them?" he asked and himself began clapping loudly. The crowd joined in slowly at first, and soon Devi and Sharmila were getting a standing ovation to thunderous applause.

The minister raised his hand for silence and asked everyone to settle down.

"Devi, we are proud of what you have achieved. Please say a few words of inspiration to all of us," said the minister.

Devi took the mike from him and took the centre-stage. "This is a very emotional moment for me," she choked. Sharmila held her hand and it took her a few seconds to regain her composure.

"I would like to thank a lot of people, please bear with me as I introduce them to you. I have two mothers – one from your world, Naina Malhotra. Mom, please come on stage."

Naina slowly walked up to the stage. Her kohl-rimmed eyes were moist and she looked like she was about to break down and cry. She stepped onto the stage looking like an angel, with her hair tonsured, so feminine and so strong.

Devi touched Naina's feet and hugged her. The audience was once again giving them a standing ovation. Flash bulbs kept going off as the photographers clicked left, right and centre. Naina just stood there, smiling, her eyes brimming with tears.

Devi took to the mike once again and said, "I have another mother, one from my world. Chandani. Maa, please come on stage."

Chandani also walked up to the stage and stood beside Devi, proud and tall. Devi touched her feet.

"I would also like to introduce a man who is not my father but has been more than my father to me; it is because of him that I am standing here, receiving this award. My Rock of Gibralter, Mr Naveen Sharma."

Naveen stood up and walked up to the stage. Devi hugged him as he kissed her forehead and the crowd cheered.

"And finally, I would like to introduce you to our entire *Trans Color* team. This company is not mine, it is ours!"

The crowd went crazy as all thirty-five of them walked onto the stage. Dressed in colorful saris, they folded their hands in Namaste and took a bow.

The minister took the mike once again. "I have no words to express my happiness at this moment. We have all had a beautiful evening, thanks to you lovely ladies. Devi, I am so proud of you. If there is anything I can ever help you with, please feel free to ask."

"I need ten minutes of your precious time, Bhishnoi sir; we would love to show our latest products to you."

The minister looked at his watch and said, "Devi, I am already running late. Ten minutes is all the time I can spare."

"Thank you sir, we won't take a minute longer."

Sharmila signalled for the lights to be dimmed as Naveen, Naina and the Minister stepped off the stage. The music started playing and Parvati walked onto the stage, leading the cat walk. They had all removed the safety pins which had kept their *pallus* folded over their blouses, concealing them. They walked one by one and in the end, held hands as Ameena came on the stage and took the final bow with them as their designer.

Naveen and Naina held hands, choking with emotion. "We did it Naina!"

Devi had become a small town celebrity. She was surrounded by the media, mikes and cameras in hand.

Naina went home that night and slept like a woman who was finally free, from the iron chains of pretence and hypocrisy. She knew Manish and she would quarrel in the morning when he read the newspaper, but she did not care anymore.

Manish did see the newspapers the next morning. He stared at the picture of Devi, standing on stage, flanked by Naina and

Chandani for a long time. But he did not say anything to Naina; Devi was Devi Sharma. He wondered where the family name came from until he saw Naveen's picture with Devi and got his answer.

He walked up to Naina and put both his arms around her. Naina was taken aback. She looked at him questioningly.

"You have a large heart, Naina. Look what you have achieved." He said pointing to the picture of Devi in the newspaper. "I am sorry for not being there for you, but I still can't bring myself to accept Devi."

"Tell me something Manish. What if we had a child who was deaf, dumb, blind or disabled? Would you not have accepted the child?"

"I don't know what I would have done."

"It's just not fair to expect your children to be like you. How can any parent stop loving their own child? You have to be there for your children, no matter what."

"I understand that logically Naina, and intellectually also. But I still cannot bring myself to accept Devi as my daughter. I just can't do it. Even the thought that people will make fun of me scares me. I don't think I can handle it. You are a strong woman Naina, and I really respect you for that, but that is it for me; nothing more."

Naina did not answer. Manish hugged her again and walked out of the room.

Naina called Chandani the next day. "We have to find a companion for Devi. This is something that I can't do."

"She has a companion in Lord Aravan, Naina."

"Yes, of course. But, she needs a human companion, Chandani."

"Aravan is kind. He will find someone for her; don't worry."

✗

Devi did find somebody at the next festival in Koovagam.

She called Naina. "I met somebody Mom and I want to get married, today itself; a small ceremony at the temple in the evening."

Naina smiled, closed her eyes for a moment and thanked Thakur ji as tears flowed from her eyes.

"Mom? Are you upset? Say something please."

"Why should I be upset? I am delighted for you."

"I am sorry that all this is happening so fast. He will come back with me after the ceremony to seek your blessings, and Dad's too."

"That's wonderful news. Ask Sharmila to click a few pictures of the ceremony and send them to me. Where is he from?"

"He's from Gujarat," she giggled. "He can understand Hindi, but is not fluent. He starts speaking in Hindi, but switches to Gujarati after two sentences. He manages all our sourcing from Gujarat. I think I will have to learn Gujarati."

Naina smiled and said bye. She called Naveen and told him about the conversation with Devi.

"Naina, at least stop crying now. I only understood the part that Devi has met somebody. The rest was all your sobs. I will talk to her, thank you." Naveen disconnected the line.

Naina called Chandani. "Spend as much as you need. I will pay for everything. Money is no object. Will she leave Jaipur?"

"No, no, she will not. He will keep visiting her. They will juggle between Rajkot and Jaipur. He is not a graduate like

Devi, but has studied till the 10th standard. He is tech-savvy, well-read and very affectionate. You will like him, Naina."

"I can't wait to see him. Tell Sharmila to send some pictures to me please By the way, you sound tired. Are you fine?"

"Not too great, Naina. I have fever again and before you start giving me a lecture about checking with a doctor, I have. He says it's viral. I am on antibiotics."

"Ok. Please take your medicines regularly."

"By the way, Devi wants to get herself castrated. She wants to get it done as soon as we come back to Jaipur."

Hijras do this to feminize themselves. When a Hijra gets himself castrated, they call it Nirwaan. Castration is strictly optional and is a personal choice of a Hijra. Devi was an intersex. She had both the genitals. Devi was getting married and she wanted to be a complete woman.

Naina was surprised, confused, horrified, all at the same time. "But why would she want to do that?"

"She wants to be a woman."

"But, she is a woman."

"She is not, Naina."

"Even I have a uterus and after some years it will be no good. But that does not mean I will get it removed. I just don't understand. Why can't she just let the penis be, it's all in her head."

"Please don't compare what's inside to what's outside one's body; moreover it is her personal decision."

Naina decided to not argue any further.

"Ok! But please tell me that we have some good doctors in Jaipur who can perform this surgery."

"I really don't know. We will have a mid-wife to do it."

"Oh my God! No! If at all she gets it done, she will go through a proper surgery. I am not letting her go under the knife just like that."

"These operations are very expensive Naina. We can't afford them."

"Not even now?" Naina asked.

"The profits from *Trans Color* are shared equally among all thirty-five of us. That is how Devi wanted it, so we cannot afford it."

"Ok, let me think about it. But Chandani, you have to promise me that you will not get it done without taking me into confidence."

"Yes, yes. Don't worry." Chandani promised.

Devi and Jignesh

☿

Naina went to the bank the next day and got all her jewellery home. She set aside the three sets her mother had given her when she had gotten married and put the rest in her locker. She then went to her jeweller and selected a gold chain to be given as shagun for when she would first meet Devi's husband, Jignesh.

When Devi returned to Jaipur, she invited Naina and Naveen to visit them. They reached the kothi in the evening when a delighted Devi introduced them to Jignesh. He was much thinner and shorter than the tall, broad Devi but had a soft, fair skin.

A woman who identified herself like a man! thought Naina and smiled.

They both bent down to touch Naina's feet. Naina gave Jignesh a blue velvet box which had the gold chain. "Can I open it please?" He asked Naina.

"Yes please, it is for you!"

He opened the box, removed the chain from the box and wore it.

"I have never seen this kind of love and support from the parents or friends of a Hijra. I feel truly blessed to have you around. I miss my parents." He said choking with emotion.

Devi put an arm around his shoulder and squeezed it gently. "We have each other now."

She then took out the three sets she had got for Devi and gave them to her. Devi opened the boxes one by one and returned them to Naina after seeing the contents saying, "No mom, I cannot accept these. This is too much. I am earning now."

To which Naina promptly replied, "Darling, if you were living with me and I would have gotten you married, I would have spent ten times of what I am giving you right now. So please keep it."

Devi hugged her and handed them over to Chandani for safekeeping. They were heavy *Jadau* sets. "They are stunning mom, thank you!"

Then it was Naveen's turn. Naveen blessed them as they bent down to touch his feet and handed them a sealed envelope. "Come on! Open it and see what's inside Jignesh."

Devi opened it and much to her surprise there were air tickets in it. "Dad, thank you, but we are not going anywhere!"

"Grow up Devi and look at the tickets carefully. Every country that you will visit is transgender friendly and your hosts will also be transgenders, so chill! It took me the whole week to plan you trip, and Naina, for God's sake, don't cry." Overcome with emotion, Devi hugged Naveen.

Naina gave two packets of laddus for everybody. She then went to Chandani, bent down and touched her feet. Chandani blessed her and said, "Now what?"

"Thank you for everything," Naina replied and gave her a beautifully packed pink and orange chiffon sari with silver *gota-patti* work on the border.

She also gave her two gold bangles which Chandani refused to accept. "I will keep the sari, but I am not going to accept the bangles."

"Please keep it mom, otherwise..." Devi began.

"NAINA WILL CRY!" everyone finished in unison. Everybody started laughing and clapping. Naina then gave a sari each to all the Hijras. All beautifully packed chiffon leheria saris and each one blessed her in turn.

"Now that Santa Claus has finished distributing gifts, let us eat something. I am hungry," said Naveen. Everybody got to work and hot tea was served with pasta.

Devi finally did get her operation done; she went through a proper surgery. Naina had insisted on it. She mortgaged one of Naina's sets and took a loan from a local jeweller for her operation.

Two months later, when everything was back to normal, Devi called Naina, "Mom, I haven't seen you in a long time, how are you?"

"All well sweetheart! How are you? Are my daughter's struggles finally over?"

"No Mom. I am a Hijra; my struggles will never be over. But you have made me strong enough to handle anything and everything that comes my way."

Naina smiled. She knew now that it was time to let her little bird fly.

That July it rained heavily in Jaipur. The thirsty desert soil soaked every bit of the water. The weather was very pleasant.

Jaipurites were enjoying the weather. The Ramgarh Lake was full of water. But somewhere in mid July, it all turned ugly. It rained for six days non-stop. Jaipur recorded an all time high of 7 mm rain. The schools were shut. There was water logging everywhere. The walled city was the worst hit. There was flooding on the streets, trees and poles were falling, blocking the roads and the new channels were reporting of traffic jams everywhere.

The sun appeared on the seventh day. The citizens of Jaipur heaved a sigh of relief.

Since there was water logging everywhere, there was a mosquitoe menace to be dealt with. There was a huge malaria scare and the government was making announcements on the television and radio to be extra careful. Patients were being rushed various hospitals for treatment. Volunteers were distributing leaflets with details regarding the prevention and cure of malaria. The municipal corporation was spraying insecticides in high risk areas.

Chandani fell ill too. She had fever accompanied with body aches. For the first two days, she ignored it. She kept popping Crocin every six hours. On the third day, she developed high fever and started vomiting and shivering. The Hijras panicked. Sharmila called Devi who was in Surat.

"She is not well at all. We are taking her to the hospital."

"What's wrong with her?"

"High fever."

"Should I come or will you be able to manage?"

"I really don't know. I shall call once I meet the doctor."

They called for an auto and rushed her to the nearest Sawai Man Singh Hospital. The emergency wing of the hospital was jam-packed. They waited for a good half an hour before the doctor attended her.

"Since when does she have fever?"

"Two days."

"Padhe likhe nahi ho kya? Why did you take so long to get her here?" he shouted.

He immediately admitted her into the ICU and asked the nurse to take her blood sample and get it examined.

Devi called Sharmila after about an hour.

"How is she?"

"They have admitted her into the ICU."

"What? What happened to her?"

"They are suspecting malaria. The blood sample has been sent for examination."

"But why did they put her in the ICU?"

"I don't know. There are too many people here. The doctor is very busy."

"Please don't worry. I will take the first available train. Forget the train, I will take a taxi."

She immediately called up Naveen.

"Dad, mom is not well. Can you please go the hospital? They have taken her to SMS. She is in the ICU."

"Who is with her? What happened to her?"

"Sharmila, please coordinate with her. She has malaria, most probably."

"Then there is nothing to panic. I will go the hospital in a while and get back to you."

Naveen called Sharmila after half an hour.

"Aap kahan ho?"

Sharmila started crying.

"Why are you crying? Relax, it's only malaria. I am on the way."

"She has gone into coma."

"What? I am coming. Give me ten minutes."

He parked his car in front of a medicine shop and ran inside.

He saw ten of them standing outside the emergency. Savitri saw him and rushed towards him.

"Come, I will take you inside."

They ran till the ICU and saw Sharmila standing outside. Naveen asked her the bed number and rushed inside to talk to the doctor.

The resident doctor briefed him about Chandani's condition.

"The reports are not in, but we are suspecting cerebral malaria. The patient is in coma."

"Is it serious?"

"Very serious. Do you know these people? I mean the Hijras?"

"Obviously, that's why I am here."

"Please wait outside. I shall inform you about any further development."

Naveen stepped out and called up his friend Dr Megha.

"Sorry for bothering you Megha, but I need some help."

"Tell me Naveen."

"Do you anybody in SMS?"

"Of course. What happened?"

Naveen explained everything to her.

"I need someone to see her and tell me exactly what's happening. There is no senior doctor available here right now. I would also like to get a second opinion if possible."

"Let me see what I can do. Give me ten minutes."

After about fifteen minutes, another doctor called up and introduced himself as a friend of Megha. He informed Naveen that he better ask the Hijras to get their affairs in order. "I spoke to the doc in the ICU. They are doing their best but the chances of her surviving are very thin."

"Is there nothing we can do, doc? Money is not an issue."

"Nothing. I am sorry. But that's the way it is. She is sixty plus. Has a very low immunity. They took too long to bring her in. The doctors might tell you that there is hope, but the truth is, it's just a matter of time. I am sorry Naveen. I am around. If I can be of any help, do let me know."

"Thanks Doc. I really appreciate the help."

✕

Chandani passed away at 6 in the evening. Devi could not meet her.

Naveen told Sharmila to inform her family. Sharmila looked at him and said, "Which family?"

Naveen bit his lip.

The Hijras took her body home. A lot of Hijras from other kothis came to pay their last respects.

There were murmurs about lighting the pyre at night or early the next morning.

Naveen stood with Naina in one corner and watched silently. They decided to wait for Devi.

She arrived at 4 in the morning. Devi was inconsolable. She hugged Naveen and wept. Naina held her hand right through. Devi touched Chandani's feet.

"Forgive me Maa, I could not be there for you." She wailed.

"What will I do without you?" Her cries resounded in the hall.

The body was taken to the cremation ground at 5.15 in the morning. The Hijras wore white kurta pyjamas sans any jewellery or make up. All the women suddenly turned men, except for their long hair which they tied in buns. Naina and Naveen exchanged glances across the hall. It was difficult to even recognize a few of them. Both of them didn't know why this was being done.

Devi torched Chandani's funeral pyre. Naina stood at a distance and watched Naveen holding Devi's hand as he torched the pyre. Is that my son Thakur ji? asked Naina.

They came back. Naveen dropped Devi to the kothi and went back home to Srishti. He promised to come back at around noon again.

Naina too left after a while.

"Why did they wear white kurta pyjamas and not saris?" asked Srishti when he reached home. "They could have worn dull saris."

"I am not sure. They probably don't want the world to know that Chandani was a Hijra. They wanted the funeral to happen at night but later decided to wait for Devi. I sure will miss Chandani. What a wonderful lady she was." Naveen sighed.

"Is Devi taking it well?"

"No, she is absolutely miserable right now."

✗

On the thirteenth day after her death, when all the ceremonies were over, all the Hijras of the Kothi gathered in the hall. The

Gurus of all the remaining kothis of Jaipur were also invited. The kothi of Haji colony now needed a new Guru.

All of them sat on the floor in silence and the Gurus sat on chairs. Jyoti, the Guru of the Sanganer kothi stood up and addressed everyone.

"We have lost Chandani. It is an irreparable loss for not just the members of Haji colony kothi, but for the entire Hijra community. She was a wonderful, loving woman. May her soul rest in peace. I hope and pray that God gives all of you the strength to bear her loss.

"This kothi needs a new Guru. Pieces of paper and pens will be distributed to all of you. Please write down the name of your preferred candidate."

Sharmila stood up and addressed everyone. She folded her hands and said, "With due respect to all the Gurus sitting here, I wish to inform you that we don't need an election."

The Gurus looked at each other. Some of them were enraged. "Then why have you invited us here?"

"Let her finish," said another Guru from the Ramganj kothi.

Sharmila continued, "To disrespect you is not my intent at all. We all want Devi as our next Guru. There is not a single person here who is opposed to my view."

Everyone agreed with her with shouts of approval.

Devi was absolutely surprised. She stood up and started sobbing. After a few minutes she gained her composure and said, "I am the youngest in this kothi, how can I be their Guru?"

There were murmurs amongst the Gurus.

"Are you saying that you don't want to be their Guru?"

"How can I take my mother's place? It is just too much responsibility."

"Is there anybody's name that you would like to propose then?"

Devi looked around. There was no one she could think of. There was no one like Chandani. She looked at Sharmila for some help. Then suddenly, it struck her. Why not Sharmila? She is the smartest of us all.

"I propose Sharmila's name," she announced.

Sharmila stood up once again. "I refuse to become the Guru. Devi is the only one who is educated amongst us. She has transformed our lives. From a group of singing, dancing Hijras, living in a state of penury, we are now a group of entrepreneurs. I have seen times when we survived on roti and onions for months because we had no money to feed ourselves. She is not just the harbinger of change, but also the change we all want to be. She has not just made us financially independent, but also earned us acceptance, respect and dignity."

Everyone including the Gurus stood up and clapped. Devi was absolutely overwhelmed.

Jignesh held her hand and whispered in her ear, "I am there for you and always will be. Go ahead and accept the proposal."

Devi wiped her tears, held Jignesh's hand and said, "Yes, I will be your Guru. But Sharmila, you have to be my guide."

Sharmila flung both her arms around her and hugged her.

Devi bent down and touched the feet of all the elders. Slowly life bounced back to normal and the Hijras got back to their routine of frenzied activity – managing sales, production and dispatches. But nothing was the same as what it was. Devi had transformed it for good!